First Dry (
Copyright © 2

Morning Cup of Murder

Vanessa Gray Bartal

Prologue

Barbara Blake was home, although she had a hard time thinking of the tiny one-horse town of her birth as "home." In fact, no place had ever felt like home, and now she knew why. She had been wrong about everything.

Never having been one to admit her mistakes easily, it had taken a long time to arrive at her conclusion. Now that she had, she wasted no time in self-recrimination. Instead, she did what she had always done: she made a plan and decided to carry it out. And this time she would do it right.

She looked around her parents' hovel with a sneer of disgust. She should really do something about this place. A pre-war bungalow, it was small, but it had good bones. If she knocked out a few walls and did an extensive renovation, it could be quite cute. But she wasn't going to do that. She had bigger fish to fry. Soon she would have something of her very own, something no one could take away from her.

When a knock sounded at the door, she smiled in gleeful triumph. *Dance, little puppets, dance,* she thought. All the players were arranged, and Barbara was about to have some fun. Unlike when she had lived here before, she now had money and power-- the two things she had craved for so long, and the two things that made the world go round. Also unlike before, she now knew how to wield them both to get what she wanted. She was just a hairsbreadth away from having it all, and no one was going to stop her-- certainly not the rubes in this town who had always done whatever she told them to do.

Barbara opened the door and her smile slipped and died. "Oh, it's you," she said with no warmth or welcome. With this person she had never had to pretend to be someone else. "What do you want?"

"Hello, Barbara. I thought we could have a little talk and catch up. For old time's sake."

1

Barbara shrugged and gave a humorless little chuckle. "Sure, why not? You can tell me all the ways your life hasn't changed." She turned and led the way inside and to the kitchen. Maybe it would be fun to play hostess for a little while. She could catch up on all the latest gossip in town. Her visitor knew everything about everyone but had never been very forthcoming with mindless chatter.

If she was really going to play the hostess bit, she should probably offer something to eat or drink. "Would you like some...?"

Her words turned to a cry of alarm as she caught the flash of a knife slicing through the air. Instinctively she put up her hands to protect her precious face and the expensive plastic surgery she was so proud of. But it wasn't her face that needed protection; it was her heart. With one sickening slash the blade was in her chest, and Barbara's life was fading away.

She sank to her knees and onto her back as death came slowly. Now the person standing over her wore a smile of triumph.

"I hate you," her visitor said. The attacker twisted the knife, and those were the last words Barbara Blake ever heard.

Chapter 1

"Bad day at the office?"

Lacy Steele looked up from her laptop and wished she could crawl under the table. Jason Cantor stood in front of her, swirling a cup of coffee and staring down at her from his superior height. Why had she decided to visit the coffee shop in jogging pants and an oversized t-shirt? Would her trace of eyeliner and lip gloss work to perk up her tired-looking face?

"The internet crashed at home," she said. A mismatched wooden chair sat opposite her. She used her foot to push it out. "Sit."

He shook his head. "I get tired of sitting in the cruiser all day. I like to stand when I can. Plus, the vest is uncomfortable when I sit. Makes it hard to breathe. Or drink." He took a sip of his coffee and stared at her in that unnerving way he had lately.

She returned his look and allowed her eyes to stray to his uniform. Hopefully he would think it was because he had called attention to his vest, and not because she had trouble taking her eyes off him. "How do you eat while you're on duty?" She allowed her eyes to linger as if she were studying the structure of his bullet-proof vest when in reality she was picturing what was underneath. Last week she happened to see him washing his car, shirtless and dripping wet. The stubborn vision refused to leave her mind, and now it leapt to the forefront. Her cheeks turned a subtle shade of pink and finally gave her reason to tear her eyes off him. She pretended to blow on her now cold coffee before taking a sip.

"I don't. I skip lunch and eat when I get home."

"Don't you get cranky? I thought it's sort of universal that men are cranky when they're hungry."

"Cranky men make intimidating cops," he answered. His flirtatious, teasing tone caused her to look at him again. Things had been strange between them ever since she returned home. The fact

3

that he was talking to her was contrary to their previous relationship when he ignored her completely and she looked down on him for being a jock. But then that had been a long time ago in high school when she was a chubby band geek and he was the king of the school. Now she was the late bloomer who finally shed her baby fat, lost her braces, and gained contacts, and he was the small town cop with devastating good looks. She still wasn't sure she was in his league. She couldn't be considered a beauty by anyone's standards, but she was interesting with her red-gold hair and green eyes.

A month ago she ran into him on the street and he looked at her like he had never seen her before, and then he looked again and his eyes had lingered in the new way she had never expected. She had no idea he was even still around here. He had been Mr. All-American--homecoming king, salutatorian, and quarterback. If she were honest with herself, it was a bit of a letdown to see him hanging around their dead-end town, barely making ends meet as a cop whose biggest responsibility was to give tickets to the passersby who drove through the highway at the edge of town. On principle she wanted nothing to do with him. She had lived in New York City, after all. She had no taste for small town boys who were most likely reliving their glory days, but despite her best intentions she found herself drawn to him, almost captivated by him. Besides his surreal good looks there was a boyish charm and sincerity she never expected to find.

But there were also her own insecurities to overcome. After all, he had spent most of their lives pretending she didn't exist. Why now was he suddenly showing some interest? Was it because there was no one else around? Or was he a player, intent on making a conquest and then moving on?

So now instead of giving in to her temptation to flirt outrageously she simply studied him as he studied her. Finally his radio crackled. A female voice spit out what sounded like random numbers, but they must have meant something to Jason because his

4

face puckered into a frown. He pressed a button on his lapel, spoke into the microphone there, and gave Lacy an upward nod.

"See you, Lacy."

"See you, Jason," she said. She watched him exit the coffee shop and get into his cruiser. Could he feel her eyes following his every move? She hoped not.

Reluctantly she dragged her attention to the words on the page. They swam indistinctly together, a mess of letters and punctuation. Freelance writing was turning out to be not as romantic as it had sounded in college. Sure, she could set her own hours, but it was a constant battle to make enough to live. Most of her days were spent trolling the internet for possibilities while her afternoons were spent in research and writing. Thank goodness for the generosity of her grandmother or Lacy might very literally be out on the street. Or living with her parents in Florida. She shuddered and tried to focus once more on the screen in front of her.

Living with her grandmother in her tiny hometown was bad enough. Living with her parents at their retirement community in Florida was akin to wearing a giant, flashing sign labeled, "Failure." At least now she had the excuse of offering her grandmother some help. The tiny sum she paid each month for rent wasn't much, but it was enough to supplement her grandmother's meager income. And Grandma enjoyed the company. Lacy knew because she told her a dozen times a day. If Lacy was being honest, she would admit she enjoyed her grandmother's company, too. Life was lonely these days with only her laptop for a companion. On the days when her college friends posted their most recent successes on a social networking site, Lacy found comfort in whatever her grandmother was baking. She didn't have to be a genius to know she was going to start packing on the pounds if she found friends in food, but for now cookies were all she had. Cookies and Grandma, she amended.

How did it come to this? she wondered. For years she had hated this town and everything it represented. It was a dead end. Everyone in high school knew that and made plans to get away. Lacy's star had

5

been brighter than some. Not only was she a gifted student, but her writing received several awards and earned her a scholarship to a prestigious university. And then came New York.

She shook her head and stood to refill her coffee. She wouldn't think about that now. She couldn't. She would simply go on putting one foot in front of the other and things would somehow work themselves out. Right? Isn't that what people always said? Good times followed bad, or so the saying went. Lacy was due for her share of good times any day now. She couldn't envision what they would look like, but she was anxious for their arrival, nonetheless.

Unbidden her thoughts turned to Jason, but she banished them as soon as they appeared. While having a fling might prove amusing, it would no doubt leave her heart in tatters. She couldn't afford to have that happen again. Having your heart ripped out twice by the age of twenty six was too much for any one person to live through. No, instead she would concentrate on figuring out her next step and in the mean time she would work to rebuild what had been lost since college.

She sat again and sighed. So much had been lost; how could she ever get it back again? Was she supposed to feel so weary at such a young age? Her friends appeared to be having the time of their lives, but Lacy felt only defeat and something like despair. The walls were closing in, and she had nowhere to go. This was officially her dead end. Could things possibly get any worse? The answer to that, of course, was a resounding yes.

Chapter 2

The threat of poverty gave Lacy the focus she needed to finish the article. She filed it with the editor and wished her payment would come immediately instead of in two to four weeks. She caught her name on the signature and grimaced. Lacy Steele. An editor once asked her if it was a pseudonym. Sadly, it was not. She readily admitted her name sounded either like a defective manufacturing material or a character from a cheap romance. What had her parents been thinking? But when she considered changing it, at least for the purpose of her career, she didn't have the heart. Her family was so proud of her. Her mother collected every story she wrote, even the obscure ones no one else read. It would crush them if she used any name other than her own.

She stretched, yawned, closed her laptop and packed it up to go home, glancing around the crowded coffee house as she did so. Her yawn was cut short by a chuckle as she took in her surroundings. Unlike the trendy coffee houses in New York this one was homey and provincial, and so were its customers. In fact she was the youngest person in the room by far. It was no wonder they were always sold out of bran muffins here. While most big city coffee locales were stuffed with laptop-toting twenty-somethings like herself, this one resembled a geriatric convention. And almost no one had intricate French or Italian drinks. All the blue and gray heads were sipping plain old coffee, reading actual newspapers, and eating their ubiquitous bran muffins. A few people caught her eye and nodded. One of them was her old high school principal, Mr. Middleton. He gave her a nod that could either be approval or disapproval, and she returned it. He was one of those people who, though elderly, could still inspire a certain amount of fear and awe by a narrowing of the eyes.

"See you tomorrow?" Peggy, the elderly cashier, said it as a question as Lacy filed past her.

"We'll see," Lacy returned. She had become such a frequent visitor that the two were almost friends now. At least they exchanged friendly pleasantries a few times a day. Lacy had the uncomfortable feeling that she was seeing her future stretch out in a dizzying array of days just like this one until she would be one of the white haired regulars, sipping her coffee and eating her bran. *No, no, no,* she told herself. Just because she didn't have a plan right now didn't mean she never would. Eventually she would think of something to do with her life and then she would do it.

Her vague life plan left her feeling restless and dissatisfied. What was she doing here? How did she wind up in the one place she swore she would never be? And, most importantly, how could she get out?

The scent of sugar and cinnamon hit her as soon as she opened the door and worked to ease some of her anxiety. And then she saw her grandma standing at the sink and she smiled. Without asking her if she was hungry her grandma cut a slice of cake and slid it onto a plate. And even if she wasn't hungry she would eat the cake. Over the years prune cake had become her number one comfort food, and her grandma knew it. For as long as Lacy could remember her grandma had used it to try and cajole her out of whatever silly sadness she was suffering, and for as long as she could remember it had always worked. How her grandmother knew when she needed it remained a mystery. She had always seemed to possess a sixth sense about Lacy's moods.

"Thanks," Lacy said, and then she tucked into the cake. It was still warm from the oven, and the caramel topping stuck first to her fork and then to her teeth. Her eyes closed as comfort washed through her. "Grandma, you're spoiling me," she said as soon as she could safely talk.

"That's what grandmas are for," her grandmother answered, and Lacy had to agree with her because she had never known different. Her grandma was soft and plump and white-haired, just like a grandma should be. And she always smelled like a combination of

8

peppermint and vanilla. All of Lacy's memories of her involved food in some way, but that was her grandmother's way. For her food was love. And the more fattening or sugar-laden the food the more she loved someone, which was probably why her grandfather had died at a rather young age from a variety of ailments all relating to high cholesterol and diabetes. One might think that knowledge would deter Lacy from eating the calorie-laced goodies, but one would be wrong. Her jeans were starting to become uncomfortably tight lately, but she still couldn't stop herself from indulging in her grandmother's treats. She told herself it was because she didn't want to hurt the sweet, sensitive woman's feelings, but in reality they just tasted too good to pass up.

"Another piece, honey?" her grandmother offered, alerting Lacy to the fact that she had practically licked her plate clean without even noticing.

Yes. "No, thank you," she made herself say, although she stared wistfully at the cake. "Maybe I'll go for a quick run before supper, Grandma." She paused on her way out of the room and turned to look back. It was their standard routine for her to ask to help with supper and her grandma always made a blustery refusal. But just as she opened her mouth she paused and studied the older woman. What was that strange, unknown expression on her face? Sadness? Concern?

"Grandma, are you okay?"

Her grandmother looked up and forced a bright smile. "Of course, honey. You go for your run now. Supper's running a little behind anyway."

"Is there…" Lacy started to say her usual, "Is there anything I can do to help?" but her grandmother cut her off with a shake of her head.

"It's all under control, honey. Go ahead and have your run. Pretty young girls like you have to stay in shape if they want to catch a man."

Lacy waited until she left the room before allowing her grimace to show. What was the older generation's obsession with marrying off everyone under the age of fifty? Some of her earliest memories were of her grandparents teasing her about boys in her class, boys she had detested at the time, but they had laughingly called them her boyfriends. It used to make Lacy furious and embarrassed. Some of those old feelings returned to the surface now. She had carefully explained to her grandmother why she wasn't ready to date anyone just yet, but her grandmother's only response had been to nod, smile and say, "I'm sure you'll find a nice young man who will change your mind."

Her thoughts muddled as she exited the house and pounded the pavement. In books and movies people ran because they enjoyed it. To Lacy those characters were far-fetched. She ran because it was the most expedient way of burning calories, but she hated every painful, burning step. Who in her right mind wouldn't hate the hard slap of concrete underfoot, the sweat trickling down her back, and the stinging stitch in her side? She had never developed a graceful stride. Instead her yellow jogging pants made her look like an injured duckling trying vainly to return to the water. The sound wheezing from her open lips didn't help matters; it was reminiscent of faint, pained quacking.

For some reason she thought of Jason and her discomfort increased. He was one of those naturally gifted athletes who made running look simple. Many times she had seen him cruising down the football field during their Friday night games in high school. Of course she had always watched from the bleachers along with the rest of the marching band. Running for exercise had never occurred to her until her freshman year of college when she suddenly tired of being chubby. Never obese by anyone's standards her extra poundage had been labeled "baby fat." Most girls that first year of college gained fifteen pounds. Lacy and her roommate, Kimber, lost that much and then some. She could still remember the first day she and Kimber decided to start jogging to lose weight. They had to stop halfway through their run, not only because they were out of shape, but also because they were laughing too hard to continue. Kimber wasn't an athlete, either.

For a few years in New York jogging hadn't been necessary. Walking everywhere was enough to keep the excess calories at bay. And then her life fell apart and she moved back home to her grandmother's waiting arms and busy kitchen. And now her pants didn't seem to want to zip all the way. So it was time to start jogging again. As much as she loathed it she would do it. Maybe she was a failure, but she didn't have to be a fat failure.

She ran for what she hoped was three miles but was probably more like two. At any rate spots were starting to pop before her eyes like sunbursts and she took that as a cue to end her jog before she passed out on the sidewalk. With her luck someone would call the cops and Jason would be the one to find her sprawled on the cement in a puddle of her own sweat like a melted ice cream cone.

"Grandma, is supper ready?" She hoped her tone didn't sound impatient. She wanted to grab a shower before they sat down to eat.

Her grandmother looked up distractedly and Lacy wasn't sure she had heard the question, but at last she waved her hand in front of her face. "Things are going slowly, dear. Go take your shower."

Lacy nodded and paused in the doorway a moment. Were the older woman's eyes red-rimmed, or was Lacy projecting her own blue mood? Her grandmother had always been a happy woman. In fact, Lacy had never seen her sad. But as she ambled to the bathroom she wondered if that was because her grandma kept her emotions hidden. If that was the case, why would she do that? Lacy poured out her heart on an almost constant basis. Why wouldn't her grandmother reciprocate? Was it because she wanted to project a "grown up" image? Maybe that had been necessary when Lacy was a child, but she was an adult now. They were roommates. Surely they should be able to share their delights and concerns in equal measure.

She resolved to say as much to her grandmother while they were eating, but when she sat down to supper she lost her nerve. After all, this was her grandmother they were talking about. The woman was and had always been larger than life to Lacy. Her sweetness, patience, tolerance and good humor were almost supernatural. And Lacy wasn't the only one to feel that way. She once asked her mother if Grandma had ever raised her voice to her growing up and her mother smiled and shook her head.

"No, Lacy. There's no one sweeter or more genuine than your grandma. She has all the love and patience of a saint." And then her mom had rolled her eyes. "You have no idea how annoying that was when I wanted to be a rebellious teenager. I could never goad her into an argument, no matter how hard I tried."

The exchange had stuck in Lacy's head because it was one of her first grown-up insights into her mother's relationship with her grandmother; the first time she realized her mother had once been somebody's little girl, just like her.

Now she studied her grandmother surreptitiously from across the table. There were definite signs of distress on her face. For one thing she was quiet. Usually they talked about little things and big things while they ate. But so far her grandmother had been mute. And her features were pulled tight in a way Lacy had never seen before.

"Grandma, is something wrong?" she asked at last.

Her grandmother looked up in surprise and pasted on a smile. "Why, no, Lacy. Everything is fine."

Lacy took a breath to question her further, but the front doorbell rang and interrupted her query. "I'll get it," she said. She dabbed at her lips with her napkin and deposited it on the table before rising to push out her chair. They weren't prone to many visitors and she thought that might account for the way her heart was pounding in her chest. Her lashes fluttered in surprise when she opened the door and saw Jason standing on the other side. He held

12

up a piece of paper and spoke before she could gather her wits enough to talk.

"Lacy, I have a warrant…"

He would have continued but she cut him off. "You're here to arrest me?" Her voice was a faint squeak.

"Not you. Her." Lacy didn't notice the other officer until he spoke and pointed behind her to her grandmother. "Lucinda Craig you're under arrest for the murder of Barbara Blake."

Chapter 3

The plainclothes detective beside Jason grew impatient with Lacy's shocked silence. He stalked past her, knocking her aside. She would have fallen except Jason put his hand to the small of her back to keep her upright.

"Jason," she began but didn't know how to continue. His hand left her back and eased up to touch her cheek.

"Lacy," he said in a whisper, but the detective interrupted him.

"Cantor, I need your cuffs," he called.

Jason shot Lacy a regretful look and left her standing in the entryway. Lacy watched while he pulled his handcuffs off his belt and finally her tongue unfroze from the roof of her mouth.

"What are you doing? You can't arrest my grandmother," she said, but they both ignored her. Her grandmother was strangely silent and subdued, but maybe she was in shock as much as Lacy was. "This is crazy." Her fear and confusion turned to anger when they continued to ignore her. "Don't you dare put handcuffs on her."

Jason's hands paused in mid-air, the cuffs dangling listlessly as he appeared to be looking into her grandmother's sweet, drawn face.

"It's policy," the detective reminded him in a crisp tone.

Jason gave one, curt nod and resumed cuffing the old woman. Lacy watched her grandmother stare dejectedly at her feet. She had always been a sweet, unassuming woman, but her lack of protest was disturbing for a reason Lacy couldn't pinpoint.

"Grandma," she tried. "Everything is going to be okay. I'm going to contact the rest of the family and we'll get this figured out." She would have kept going but her grandmother interrupted her.

"No," she said. Her voice was faint because she was staring at her feet. She raised her head and when Lacy saw her eyes she sucked a breath and stumbled backwards a step. Her grandmother looked angry, angrier than Lacy had ever seen her. "I don't want the rest of

14

the family to know a word about this, Lacy. Promise me you won't call anyone."

"I," Lacy started, but before she could agree to the promise the detective grasped her grandmother's arm and led her from the house. "Grandma," she cried. To her annoyance and embarrassment her voice broke; tears threatened to spill over. Jason hung back, waiting until the detective left the house, and then he spoke.

"Follow us to the jail. Once the booking is done we'll have more information for you." He took a step toward the door, then paused and turned back to her. "I'm sorry," he muttered, and he exited the house, leaving the door standing open in his wake.

A fly buzzed in through the open door, and that small action was the catalyst needed to propel Lacy forward. She walked out of the house in a stunned, zombie-like way and went back inside when she realized she lacked purse and keys. It took a moment of mindless rummaging in her room until she located them and then she exited the house again, making sure to close the door behind her this time. The quiet hum of her grandmother's car felt jarring to her overwrought nerves.

The next thing she knew she was at the county jail with no memory of having driven there. She sat in her car a moment, gathering her senses and feeling dazed. Never in a million years did she imagine she would be at the jail trying to fix the mix-up that landed her grandmother in handcuffs. That thought gave her the anger she needed to burst from her car. Someone was going to pay for this colossal mistake.

Slamming her car door felt good. She wanted to repeat the process with the entry door, but it was too heavy. It closed behind her with an unsatisfyingly gentle swish.

"Who's in charge?" she demanded before quickly realizing no one was there. Her frustration inched up another notch. If she was going to take out her frustration on random strangers, the least they could do was have the courtesy to be present.

Looking around she noted a glassed-in area in the far corner with what looked like a doorbell in front of it. She used the hem of her shirt to cover her finger before touching the button, imagining the sort of people who usually came to the jail. Her nose was still wrinkled in disgust when a tired-looking young man in a uniform stepped in front of the glass.

"I'm here for my grandmother," she said, still not believing the words coming out of her mouth.

"Name," he said. His bored tone told her he couldn't care less who she was there for, or why.

"Lucinda Craig." Her voice choked embarrassingly on her grandmother's name. *Hold it together; be strong.* Always before her grandmother had been the stalwart protector. Having the shoe on the other foot was a disconcerting change of pace. Lacy suddenly felt very young and vulnerable.

The officer turned and left the window without a word. Lacy leaned forward with a scowl, trying to see where he was going, but the heavy metal door he entered impeded her vision. She jumped when the door clanged. How did anyone ever get used to that chilling sound?

The officer returned a few minutes later, looking slightly less bored and harassed. "You'll have to come back during visiting hours tomorrow," he said.

"Why?" Lacy asked.

"Because visiting hours are over for the day," he said.

"But I want to see my grandmother," Lacy said. "Please."

The guy, who looked disconcertingly younger than her twenty-five years, softened slightly and leaned forward. "Look, it's not up to me. They're questioning her right now, and that will probably go on for awhile. The detective in charge said she is absolutely not allowed to have visitors tonight, but you can come tomorrow during regular hours from ten to noon."

She wasn't sure which she wanted to do more---scream or cry. Right now crying had a slight advantage. Embarrassing tears

16

started to well behind her eyes, and she turned away, staring at a door marked "omen." Her imagination ran away with her, telling her the inability to see her grandmother tonight was a bad omen. Then she realized it was a bathroom and someone had peeled the "W" off the women's sign.

I have to get out of here before I lose it completely, she thought. She muttered her thanks to the jailer without turning around and then bolted for the exit, pushing hard against the heavy outer door. As soon as she stepped through the door, large droplets of rain pelted her face. She looked up, allowing the fat plops of water to take the place of the tears she hadn't let fall.

"You know it's raining."

Lacy had no idea how long she had been standing with her eyes closed, head tipped toward the sky, but Jason now stood in front of her, his cruiser parked a few feet away across the sidewalk. Wiping the moisture off her face while scowling at him wasn't easy, but somehow she succeeded. The rain petered out as the small cloudburst moved on.

Jason held up his hands in surrender. "Lacy, I'm not the enemy here."

Her rational mind told her that was true, but she still had no desire to talk to him or anyone else. Especially someone who was wearing a uniform. She needed to be alone to think, to process what had just happened, and to plan her next move. Pivoting on her right foot, she tried to sidestep him, but he stepped in front of her. "Hey, ease up. Let's go somewhere and grab some supper. We'll talk about it."

She stopped short, realizing he might have information she wanted. Still, she remained sullen and stubborn. "I already ate."

"Then get something to drink. Come on; you look like you're in shock. I can't send you home like this."

"I don't want to ride in that." She pointed behind him.

He turned to glance at his cruiser. "I have my car. Just give me a second to park this." He started to walk toward his cruiser but paused. "Don't leave."

She crossed her arms over her chest and shifted her weight from one foot to another. At any other time she might have worried about her hair and makeup--which were nonexistent after her run and shower. But not now. Now she was too worried and shocked to think of anything other than how to fix her grandmother's situation. At the very least Jason might be able to offer her some advice about what her next move should be.

She had no idea how long it took him to park his car and return to her; time had lost meaning for her. Everything felt hazy, as if she were looking through a fog. A part of her brain realized she was in shock. She could only hope the fog would fade enough for her to be able to think clearly about what needed to be done.

"Come on," Jason said, prompting her to fall into line beside him. "Where do you want to go?"

"Don't care," she muttered. "Whatever sounds good to you."

They stopped short in front of his car--a sporty-looking Jeep. The sight of the convertible vehicle without its top worked to jog her out of her stupor. "This is not going to go well for my hair," she muttered. She noted with surprise that he was standing beside her. He opened her door and took her hand to help her into the tall car. "Thanks," she said, blinking rapidly to try and clear her head a little more. Who knew Jason was the type of guy who opened car doors?

Since the inside of the car was dry, she guessed the car must have been parked in the covered garage behind the jail. Glancing around the interior of the car, she noticed a pencil in the console between them. "Can I use this?" she asked.

"Sure," he said. He darted her a curious glance that turned into a stare. He watched, entranced, while she wound up her long hair and fastened it with the pencil. "I've only seen that done on television," he said.

He sounded so awed that she laughed. He smiled at her and started the car. "You're not up for a crowd, are you?" he guessed.

"Not really," she said.

He nodded. "I have an idea." He pulled out of the jail parking lot without another word, heading she knew not where.

Conversation was impossible while he drove. Without the top on the Jeep, the wind whistled and slashed around them, roaring in her ears. Though it was summer, the sun was setting, and the night air was beginning to turn cool. Goosebumps rose on her arms, but she did nothing to try and chafe the warmth back into them. The cold air helped clear her head so that by the time they arrived at the fast food restaurant, she was almost feeling normal.

"What do you want?" Jason asked as he turned into the drive-thru.

"Nothing," she replied. "I already ate."

"Drink something," he commanded. Turning toward the speaker, he ordered a soda for her along with a burger meal for himself. They remained silent while he paid for the food, and then they were driving again. Their small town thinned out, giving way to the rolling countryside. Seeing the dusky pastures through the open Jeep was somehow soothing. Lacy had never considered herself a convertible type person, but she was rethinking things. Maybe when she could afford a car she would invest in something with a pop-top. Then she would move somewhere warm. Somewhere sane, where old ladies weren't arrested for nothing.

Renewed thoughts of her grandmother's predicament meant she was frowning when they pulled off the road and parked. Absently, she noted a few other cars parked several feet away. She looked around, trying to see what the attraction was that drew people here, but there was nothing but the last vestiges of the sun setting behind a hill.

"Thank you," she replied automatically when Jason handed her a soda. She sipped in silence and watched while he downed his burger in record time.

He gave her a sheepish smile as he wiped his fingers with a napkin. "I haven't eaten since breakfast this morning. I was starving," he explained.

"It's not good for you to go so long without eating," she said.

"Duly noted," he replied. "You want to talk about it?" He aimed the napkin toward the open food bag, lobbing it like a basketball and smiling smugly when it easily bounced in.

Lacy set her soda in the cup holder.

"You going to finish that?" Jason asked.

"Help yourself." She passed it into his open hand, waiting to speak until he took a sip and set it aside. "I don't understand how anyone in his right mind could think my grandmother is a murderer. She's the sweetest person in the entire world."

"Murderers don't have a type," Jason said.

"Jason," Lacy exclaimed. "This is my grandmother we're talking about. She's the epitome of innocence. She thinks it's a sin to say 'heck' and 'darn.' Someone would have to be a sociopath to murder whoever they said she murdered and then come home and bake her granddaughter a prune cake. It's just not possible."

"We wouldn't have arrested her if the evidence wasn't compelling," Jason said. By his calm, neutral tone she couldn't tell if he was arguing with her or simply playing devil's advocate.

"What is the evidence?"

"I can't tell you," he said.

She threw up her hands in frustration. "Then why did you bring me here?"

"Because you looked like you were going to drive off a cliff if I let you go home alone."

"What *can* you tell me?"

"The woman who was murdered was named Barbara Blake."

"I already knew that," Lacy said. "That rude detective said it when he arrested my grandmother. Who was she? How was she murdered? When was she murdered?" Her mind turned somersaults, trying to think up an alibi for her grandmother. If the murder

20

happened during the night, there was no way her grandmother would have been able to sneak out unnoticed. Lacy's room was right next to the garage.

Jason's blank expression infuriated her further. "Let me guess: you can't tell me," she said. He shook his head. "I think you're on a power trip like that detective," she accused.

His lips pressed into a grim line. "Don't ever compare me to Detective Brenner. I'm not a detective; I'm not even a sergeant. I'm a peon who does what I'm told, regardless of how I feel about it. The law is the law, and I'm sworn to follow it."

She sat back slightly and tilted her head to inspect him. He had changed into a pair of khaki shorts and a polo shirt. The shirt clung to his muscled chest, outlining every sinew. A part of her mind recognized the fact that he looked good enough to eat with a spoon, but she ignored the thought. "Are you telling me you don't think my grandmother is guilty?"

"I didn't say that. It's not for me to decide guilt or innocence. I can only carry out the law as it's written."

She blinked at him. "Jason, who talks like that?"

He grinned at her and reached over to pinch her bicep. "I do, and I'm surprised you don't, big city writer girl."

She sat back again, crossing her arms over her chest. "I'm not a writer all the time. I have a life outside my job."

"I don't," he said.

"Why not?" she asked. How could someone who looked as good as him not have a fabulous life, even if he did remain stuck in their tiny town?

"I work odd hours. And, really, who is there to hang out with? The few people who remain from high school are stoners who I usually end up arresting once a month. And then there's you." Now it was his turn to sit back and study her. "What are you doing here, Lacy? I thought New York was your dream."

"It was," she said.

"Then why did you come back?"

She didn't want to talk about it, especially not with Jason. She shrugged, aiming for nonchalance. "Plans change."

He smiled again. "Mysterious."

She quirked an eyebrow at him. Her? Mysterious? Was he teasing her, or was he actually curious about her life? As far as she was concerned, the less he knew, the better. He picked up her soda again and took a few sips. She used the silence to scan the horizon once more. And then she sat up in alarm, looking down the row of cars beside them.

"Jason, do you know where we are?" She turned to look at him and saw him grinning at her again, clearly amused.

"How do *you* know where we are?" he asked. "Have you been here before?"

"Everyone in town knows where makeout point is," she said.

"What an interestingly evasive answer," he said. He leaned back slightly, lacing his fingers behind his head. "Who did you date in high school? I can't remember."

"Who *didn't* you date in high school? I can't remember."

His smile widened. "You. I didn't date you."

There was a sudden atmospheric shift between them, and she wasn't sure if it was because he was making fun of her or flirting with her. Was he reminding her of the difference in their social status during high school, or was he hinting that he wanted to date her now? Nervously, she glanced around again. "Do you come here often?"

"Every night," he said, "when I'm on duty. I like to think I'm doing my part to keep the town's teen pregnancy rate in check by putting the fear of God into these kids."

"Is that why we're here now? To frighten children?" She had the sudden vision of them banging on windows, scaring pimple-faced teenagers into celibacy. Strangely, the thought wasn't repulsive to her. Maybe she truly wanted to keep kids on the path of righteousness, or maybe there was a hidden part of her that wanted to take a power trip.

22

"No, that's not why we're here." His warm tone caused her to look up at him in alarm. Surely he wasn't suggesting they should make out, was he? Her heart started to thump painfully again. "It's a pretty view," he added, quelling her quaking nerves back into submission.

"It is that," she agreed. They both faced forward to watch the last few rays of sunlight dissolve into the horizon.

"I've been watching you since you came back," he announced into the sudden silence.

"Creepy stalker, party of one, your table is ready," she replied.

He ignored her. "You're interesting. You keep to yourself, but you're observant. You watch people. I can't figure out what's going on in your head. And you're funny, even when you're not trying to be." She frowned at that, but he didn't notice.

"Something happened in New York, something that hurt you," he continued. Apparently she wasn't the only observant one in the car. "No comment?" he asked, glancing at her out of the corner of his eye.

She remained stoic, enjoying the opportunity to have a legitimate reason to stare at him. He was so very pretty with his chiseled jaw, kaleidoscope eyes, and long, dark lashes.

She wondered if he read the attraction she felt for him because he swallowed hard and cleared his throat uncomfortably. "I didn't expect you to be interesting," he commented. "I don't remember you as being interesting before you went away. And I don't remember..." He broke off and looked away, almost like he was embarrassed.

"Don't remember what?" she asked. Why did he have to stop talking just when he seemed to be getting to the good part?

"I should get you home," he said. He started the Jeep and pulled out of the lot, effectively cutting off any further communication. He pulled up behind her car, still parked in the jail lot. "I'll follow you home," he said.

"Jason, what should I do about my grandma?" she asked.

23

"Hire a good lawyer," he said.

She frowned, instantly furious with him all over again. "She didn't do it."

He shrugged. "If Detective Brenner thinks she did, then he'll do everything in his power to keep her in jail. She needs a lawyer, Lacy. A good one."

Lacy felt like crying and was suddenly desperate to get away from him before her tears could start. She fumbled for the latch on the seatbelt a few times before realizing it was stuck.

"That happens sometimes," he said. He leaned over her and pressed the release button. When it didn't budge, he released his own belt and moved closer, placing both arms over her to try and reach the belt.

Why does he have to smell so good she wondered. Female criminals must throw themselves at his feet, asking to be handcuffed.

"This thing is really jammed," he said. "There." The latch popped free. He looked up at her with a smile and froze, very close to her face. "Sorry about that," he whispered.

"It's okay," she assured him. She had no idea why they were whispering.

"I've never seen someone with red hair and no freckles," he said. His eyes skimmed her face before resting on her lips.

"Glad I could be the first," she said. He was so close and so pretty. Never before had she been this physically attracted to someone. Previously she had prided herself on valuing a man's mind over his body. Personality and intelligence had always been at the top of her list of requirements. Now she began to see why some women went for looks. Jason's handsome face and well-cut physique made her weak-kneed and addlebrained. When she realized she was the one who put her hands on his shoulders and began to close the distance between them, she came to a sudden stop and jerked back against the car seat. Jason, who apparently came to his senses at the same moment, jumped away from her as if she were a puff adder.

In his haste to get away from her, he hit the steering wheel, causing the horn to beep. The loud sound shattered the stillness, making her already frazzled nerves dance. She jumped down from the car, stumbling a step and using the driver's side mirror to steady her balance.

"Okay?" he asked, his tone clipped.

"Okay," she replied. "Thanks for the lift." She didn't look back as she practically ran to her car. She wished he wouldn't follow her home. She wanted to take a few minutes to rest her head against the steering wheel and gather her senses. Instead she drove home on autopilot, let herself in the door, and waved to let him know she was okay.

Once his Jeep was out of sight, she leaned against the door, slid to a sitting position on the floor, and rested her head on her knees. What was wrong with her? She had vowed to have nothing to do with men ever again, and now she had almost kissed a *Jason*. He was everything she didn't want in a man--cocky, too handsome, a small town guy, and irritatingly out of her league. If she ever decided to date again, she wanted a nice man who was smart and could make her laugh. If he wasn't horrible on the eyes that would be a bonus, but not a necessity. No matter what, she vowed not to get involved with Jason Cantor. But even as she made the vow, there was a part of her mind that was busy continuing their aborted kiss attempt. How would it feel to kiss Jason Cantor? He was and had always been the nicest-looking guy of her acquaintance and she, Lacy Steele, had come *this close* to kissing him. With a groan of frustration she closed her eyes and let her skull thump against the door.

Chapter 4

Lacy was sure she wouldn't be able to sleep. Thoughts of the confusing evening with Jason as well as the heartbreaking vision of her grandmother rotting in jail were certain to keep her up all night. But they didn't; she slept well and soundly, only waking the next morning when the phone began to ring.

"Hello," she said, reaching blindly for the jangling instrument and speaking into the wrong end.

"Miss Steele, this is Ed McNeil. I run a law firm in town, and I hear your grandmother is in need of my services."

Lacy adjusted the headset, frowning into the correct end now. Ed McNeil was a familiar name in this town. He was a smarmy ambulance chaser, always defending guilty criminals who found themselves on the wrong end of the law. The police hated him. Other lawyers resented him. Even the people he defended disliked him because his fees were so steep, even though he was usually successful at getting them off.

"No, thank you," Lacy said sleepily. "I have someone else in mind."

"Now, ma'am, from what I hear, your grandmother doesn't stand a snowball's chance. I'd say I'm your last hope. You don't really want to turn me away."

Her frown deepened to a scowl. Was that true? Was this oily creature her grandmother's only hope? No. Truth would prevail; and, more importantly, she didn't want her family associated with this man and his unethical defense tactics. "No thank you," she restated more firmly.

"But I really think…"

She hung up on him. The phone rang again. She let it go to her grandmother's old-fashioned answering machine, guessing correctly that it would be Ed McNeil again. He left an obnoxiously long message, extolling his own virtues and reiterating that her grandmother had no hope without him.

When the phone rang again, she let that go, too. Another lawyer from the McNeil firm left another depressing, desperate message.

"Ambulance chasers," she muttered. Throwing off her covers, she stumbled to the shower. She emerged clean, but not refreshed. A glance at the clock showed her why; it was only seven in the morning.

As she passed by the answering machine in the kitchen, she saw that three more messages had come in while she was showering and she didn't need to press "play" to know who they were from. The phone rang again, and she turned off the ringer.

She had three hours to kill before she could visit her grandmother. Now was the time to gather information. Grabbing her laptop, she returned to the coffee shop that had become her second home. As usual, the place was filled with a dozen blue hairs. On almost every plate was a large bran muffin.

"Hi, Lacy." Peggy the cashier's tone was sympathetic when it was Lacy's turn in line. "You're here early today."

"Coffee, please. And a muffin."

"We're out of bran," Peggy said.

Lacy stifled the unbidden urge to laugh. "Chocolate chip will be fine. That's my favorite."

"Mine too," Peggy said conspiratorially. "Although when you get to by my age, you start giving up the things you love for the things that are good for you." She set a muffin on a plate, poured a coffee from the pot, and slid them across the counter. They exchanged money, and Lacy turned to go.

The line behind her was still long. She had to pivot around several of the town's elderly who made no move to get out of her way. She sat at a tiny table not far enough from civilization to suit her. Jason's comment from the night before came to mind. *You keep to yourself.* Did she really? Did people view her as standoffish? New

York had taught her to mind her business, but she never lost her insatiable curiosity about the world around her.

She slumped over her muffin feeling suddenly defeated. Maybe she was depressed. Her life had certainly become depressing. Where was the joie de vivre she had once felt? When had excitement over her future been replaced by pessimism? Was she doomed to repeat this muffin-consumption routine until she died? Was her life out of surprises?

Her computer came to life, offering a blessed reprieve from her sad introspection. As soon as she cleared up this mess with her grandmother, she was getting out of this town. Nothing good or interesting ever happened here. What Lacy needed was a shot of excitement, stat.

The town's only newspaper came to life on the screen. The main headline screamed something about the county fair next week. It took Lacy less than a minute to discover the story she was looking for. "Woman Found Dead in Home," the headline read. But a click of the link showed nothing more than Lacy already knew.

"Barbara Blake was found dead in her home yesterday. Police are still investigating."

That was it; that was the extent of the story. After a few seconds of stunned disbelief, Lacy threw down the remainder of her coffee and muffin, gathered her laptop, and stormed out of the café.

The beauty of a small town was that everything was within walking distance to everywhere else, which was good because Lacy didn't have a car. Occasionally she borrowed her grandmother's car, but she tried not to do that often, hating to be more dependent on her family than she had to be. She didn't mind walking; she had grown used to it in New York where public transportation made a private vehicle unnecessary.

The newspaper was three buildings from the coffee shop. Lacy walked inside and impatiently drummed her fingers on the counter as she waited for someone to notice her presence and offer help.

28

Eventually a large woman stood and sashayed to the desk. "Can I help you?" She sounded bored. Or tired. Or both.

"I would like to see the editor, please."

"Do you have an appointment?"

Lacy looked around the tiny, empty building. "Are you kidding me?"

"Yes," the woman answered. Turning to look over her shoulder, she yelled, "Len, some girl for you." Without waiting for a reply, she turned and waddled back to her chair. Lacy was almost certain the chair groaned when the woman sat down.

A balding middle aged man--Len?--poked his head outside an office. "What?" he snapped, frowning as he looked Lacy up and down.

"I came to talk to you about the murder story in the paper this morning. Or rather, the lack of a story. I cannot believe that an actual murder in this tiny town got exactly two lines of coverage."

"The story broke last night after we were closed," he said wearily.

"And no one was willing to work overtime to report on it?"

"No," he said sharply. "For what I'm able to pay, no one was willing to work overtime. Not even for a murder." Turtle-like, he withdrew his head back into his office.

"Wait," Lacy called.

Again his head poked out of the office while his body remained hidden inside. "What?"

"I'm a writer."

"Good for you." The head began to withdraw again and Lacy hastened to continue.

"I could write the story freelance and you can pay me by the word."

The head paused, considering. "I pay less than average."

"Shocking," she said dryly.

He actually smiled at that. "All right. Have at it."

"So, just to confirm, if anyone calls you and asks if I'm a reporter working for the paper, you'll cover me," she said.

"Look, kid, we aren't Woodward and Bernstein. No one's going to call. No one's going to care."

"They'll call. They'll care," she said confidently. "I plan to rattle a few cages."

"Rattle away," he said, looking a little less bored. "What's your name?"

"Lacy Steele."

He tipped his head to the side, regarding her, but before he could ask the inevitable question, she cut him off.

"No, that's not a penname."

He smiled for the first time and she noticed his teeth overlapped each other in the front. "The deadline is three o'clock. Good luck, Steele."

With an upward nod, she turned and left the office. Now what? Recalling Journalism 101, she tried to think like a reporter. *Who, what, when, where, and why always must be answered.* Her professor's words rang in her head, providing her with a starting point. Who was Barbara Blake? That seemed like the easiest and most expedient question to answer right now.

Heading toward the library on the edge of town, she began to expand on the list of questions that needed to be answered. In addition to answering who the woman was, Lacy needed to determine how she had been murdered, when, where, and why. Without a doubt, the why would be the hardest part. If she could answer that, she could provide a motive for the murderer, essentially clearing her grandmother.

She checked her watch. It was eight. Visiting hours for the jail were in two hours. She had a ton of work to do before then.

Unfortunately when she reached the library, she realized it didn't open until nine. Sitting on the front steps, she took out her laptop and Googled Barbara Blake. When a few million hits popped up, she added the name of their town to the search. To her delight an old article from the newspaper popped up.

"*Barbara Blake, pictured center, was recently crowned our school's new homecoming queen. Surrounding her from the left are her court, Rose Greenly, Janice Harpest, Maya Grant, and Gladys Harwell.*"

Lacy checked the date on the article. The accompanying black and white picture was from Barbara's senior year, making her two years younger than Lacy's grandmother. It was improbable, though not impossible, that the two had been friends in high school. The other names, though, struck a chord with Lacy. Rose, Janice, Maya, and Gladys were some of her grandmother's best friends from her church. Together they formed the church's social committee. Since the church was comprised of so many elderly people, their main task as a group was usually arranging funeral dinners.

Since she had time to kill, she began Googling her grandmother's friends. As she had suspected, all their maiden names matched up with the girls in the picture.

Lacy stared into space, considering. What were the chances that her grandmother's friends had all been on the homecoming court with the dead woman but that her grandmother hadn't known her? Not good. There was a strong likelihood that her grandmother had known the dead woman. If they knew each other, that made proving her grandmother's innocence more difficult. It also meant Lacy would need to learn as much as she could about any possible connection between her grandmother and the dead woman.

There was one easy way to do that. She picked up her phone and pressed a button. Her mother's chipper voice cut through her anxiety, causing her to smile in spite of herself. "Hey, hon, you're up early. Is something wrong?"

Lacy thought of her grandmother's directive not to tell the rest of the family about her predicament. For now, she would honor that request. "No, Mom. I just had a question for you."

"Fire away," her mother commanded.

"Have you ever heard grandma mention a woman named Barbara Blake?"

"Barbara Blake," her mother repeated a few times. "No, the name doesn't ring a bell. Why don't you ask her?"

"It's sort of a sticky situation."

"Are you planning a surprise?" Her mother was a tenderhearted optimist who always assumed the best.

"Not really, Mom. I was just wondering."

"Have you talked to Riley?"

Lacy's smile faltered. "No."

"Lacy, she's your sister."

Her mother would have said more, but Lacy cut her off. "I should probably go, Mom. I have a few things I need to do."

Her mother's sigh was loud and expressive. "All right. Give my love to Grandma."

"I will. Love you, Mom." Lacy's voice broke on the last word.

"Lacy, are you…"

"Gotta go, Mom." She closed the phone and took a steadying breath. *Keep it together,* she warned herself. There was too much to do to let herself fall apart now.

The large clock on the front of the library told her she still had half an hour before opening time, plenty of time for her to call on one of her grandmother's friends. She thought of the list from the picture and quickly decided on the one who lived in town--Gladys Smith, nee Harwell.

As she had expected, Gladys was wide awake when Lacy knocked on her door.

"Why, Lacy, honey, what are you doing here? Is everything okay?"

Was it possible that she hadn't yet heard the news? Lacy was under the impression that the gossip in this town ran faster than the speed of light. "Not really, Mrs. Smith. I don't know how to tell you this, but Grandma has been arrested."

32

Gladys paled, gasped, and pressed her hand to her heart. "What on earth for?"

"For murder," Lacy said.

Gladys blinked at her. Lacy watched as the astonishment turned to understanding. "Well that's just not possible," she said unconvincingly.

"That's what I think. Is it possible to come in for a few minutes and talk? I have some questions."

"Oh, well, I..." Gladys broke off and looked behind her. "I have a lot going on right now."

"Please," Lacy pled. "It will just take a moment."

"Okay," Gladys agreed. If Lacy hadn't been so intent on her purpose, she would have winced at the resignation in Gladys's tone. She followed the older woman down the hallway to her frilly, lace-inspired living room. Plastic lined all the furniture and lampshades, causing a squeaking sound as Lacy sat. She was glad she had arrived early. The day was supposed to be a scorcher; it wouldn't do to get stuck to the plastic. Absently she wondered if Gladys had ever had to call the fire department to have someone peeled off her couch.

"I was wondering what you could tell me about Barbara Blake."

"Who?" Gladys's eyes darted frantically around the room, looking anywhere but at Lacy.

"The woman Grandma is accused of murdering."

"I don't think I know her," Gladys said, staring blankly at the unlit television.

"You were on the homecoming court with her your senior year of high school. I just saw the picture."

Gladys's cheeks flushed a dark shade of red at having been caught in her lie. "Oh, that Barbara Blake. I was thinking of someone else. Um, yes, we were schoolmates, but I haven't seen her in years." Suddenly she looked from the television to Lacy. "Did you just say Barbara is dead? Murdered?" All previous color was now gone from her face. In fact, she looked in danger of swooning.

Lacy nodded. "Yes, and they think Grandma did it. Obviously you know that's not possible. Please, Gladys, anything you can tell me will be helpful."

"There's really nothing to tell, Lacy." Gladys pulled out a handkerchief and mopped her forehead. "Barbara moved away soon after high school. We lost contact. I know nothing about her. Nothing."

"Were she and my grandmother friends?"

"No. Barbara was our age, and we didn't become friends with your grandmother until we were older and out of school. Barbara was long gone by then."

Lacy almost smiled at this news. If her grandmother hadn't known Barbara, then proving her innocence would be a cinch. "Can you think of any reason my grandmother would be implicated in this murder?"

"No," Gladys said, dabbing at her forehead once more.

Lacy stood to go, but instinct made her ask one more question. "Gladys, is there anything else you can tell me about Barbara?"

"Like what?" Gladys asked, her voice faint.

"What was she like?"

"I haven't known her for years, dear."

"What was she like in high school?"

For a moment, Gladys's features closed up and became hard. "She was the worst, most selfish, calculating and conniving person I've ever met," she said. Then she took a deep breath and began fanning herself with her handkerchief. "Now I really do have to get back to what I was doing." Contrary to her statement, she remained seated, staring at the television.

"Okay," Lacy said. "Thank you. And if you think of anything else, please call me."

Gladys nodded. "Don't worry about Lucinda," she said. "There's no way your grandmother killed Barbara. She had no motive."

34

Lacy turned toward the door with a frown. *What an odd thing to say,* she thought before she let herself out. But at least she had added two vital pieces of information to the puzzle: her grandmother didn't know Barbara, and Barbara hadn't lived here her whole life. Unfortunately, there were now more questions to answer. Why had Barbara moved? Where did she go? Why and when did she return? And why did she retain her maiden name? Hadn't she ever married?

And, most importantly, why had Gladys looked so nervous at the mention of the dead woman? Lacy made a mental note to contact all the other women in the picture. Maybe one of them would be more forthcoming. If not, then maybe she would have to apply a little more pressure. After all, her grandmother's life depended on it.

Chapter 5

Just as Lacy reached the library again, her phone rang. Almost before she could say hello she heard the now-familiar voice of Ed McNeil.

"Miss Steele, I wondered if you've had time to consider my offer to represent your grandmother. Lawyers like me don't stay available for long. Any minute now I expect to get another case, and then I won't be available for your grandmother. It's now or never."

"I'm going to go with never," Lacy said. She hung up and turned off her phone before he could argue. She was livid with rage. The nerve of that man! Did he have no shame? No wonder there were so many lawyer jokes. Counting the messages she knew about, he had tried to contact her six times in the past two hours. Maybe some people respected his persistence, but Lacy didn't; she found his unwavering attitude obnoxious.

Entering the library worked to cool some of her frustration. The quiet, peaceful atmosphere always had a calming effect on her. In order to expedite her research, she enlisted the help of the reference librarian who showed her where to search for the town's vital records.

Barbara Blake was seventy years old--exactly two years younger than Lacy's grandmother. She had been born in town. Sadly, her parents both died when she was in high school, leaving their house to their only daughter. The house on Chestnut Street had remained in Barbara's possession for almost the last fifty years.

Why would she keep a house she didn't live in? Lacy wondered. Was it because she still had ties to the community? If so, what were they? What had brought the woman back after so long an absence?

After having found everything she could at the library, Lacy closed her bag and exited the building. Turning right on Main Street, she headed toward Chestnut. She was suddenly insatiably curious about the house this woman had held onto for so long. Had it also been the place of her demise?

That question was answered as soon as Lacy came within sight of the building. Yellow police tape outlined the perimeter of the house, denoting it as a crime scene. Lacy ducked under a piece of tape, lightly darted up the porch steps, and peered in a window. The house was dark and the outside sunlight was bright; she couldn't see a thing.

She itched to go inside, but the sound of a weed trimmer alerted her to the presence of neighbors. No doubt if she let herself in someone would call the police. Just in case there was someone inside, she knocked on the door and rang the doorbell. No one answered. With a sly glance at the horizon, Lacy reached out and tried the doorknob. It was unlocked. The temptation to slip inside was almost too much, but she refrained. If she decided to search the house, she would come back after dark when no one was watching. Undoubtedly breaking and entering was a crime, but desperate times and all that.

Her watch alarm beeped, startling her. She had set it to go off in time for visiting hours at the jail. Tossing her bag onto her back, she began to jog down the street toward her house, noting as she ran how long it took.

Ten minutes later, she arrived on her grandmother's doorstep. She would have to drive to the jail; eight miles of country road was too far to walk in this heat. As she let herself in the front door and walked to the garage, she passed by the answering machine in the kitchen. Ten messages blinked at her. She paused, deciding to play them in case there was some news about her grandmother, but then quickly lost patience. Every message was from Ed McNeil or one of his flunky employees. There was even a young-sounding guy who suggested they go for a date to talk about Ed's talents as a lawyer.

"Disgusting jerk," Lacy muttered. She stabbed the erase button repeatedly until the machine was clear. When the phone immediately rang again, she growled, grabbed the keys by the door, and ran out without waiting to hear who the message was from. If she heard one more message from the obnoxious Mr. McNeil, she wouldn't be held responsible for her actions.

She arrived at the jail promptly at ten, but there was already a line at the jail visitation window. The same jailer whom she had met yesterday stood at the window, buzzing people through after they answered a couple of questions. At last it was her turn, and she was surprised when the guy offered her a friendly smile.

"Hey, you're back," he said.

She gave him what she hoped was a polite smile. She really wasn't in the mood for small talk, especially not from a guy who still looked pubescent. Were they hiring kids directly from high school now? "I'm here to see…" she began, but he interrupted her.

"You're here to see your grandmother. I remember." He looked around and leaned in close to the window. "We treated her well last night. She got her own cell away from everyone else. She was as comfortable as she could be; I checked."

"Thank you," Lacy said sincerely, swallowing a lump. Envisioning her precious grandmother spending the night in a jail cell was painful, even if she had been treated well.

"She's a sweet lady," the guy said. "Very polite and friendly."

Lacy nodded, blinking back tears. The guy, whose nametag read "Travis," cleared his throat. "Go through the metal door and turn left. I'll buzz them to let her know you're here."

"Thank you," Lacy said shakily. She took a deep, steady breath, waited for the door to buzz open, and then walked through, jumping slightly when it clambered shut behind her. She would never get used to that horrible sound.

As she sat in the uncomfortable plastic chair, she clasped her hands together to stop their trembling. She wasn't afraid to be here; she was afraid she would fall apart at the sight of her grandmother in an orange jumpsuit like all the other prisoners. Her grandmother--

who hadn't worn pants a day in her life--now had to wear an ugly cotton pantsuit with a number on it. It was almost too much to bear.

The minutes ticked and Lacy's anxiety grew. *What's taking so long?* she wondered.

At last the door opened, but her grandmother didn't walk through. Instead it was Travis. He sat down opposite her and picked up the phone. She did likewise and listened as he spoke.

"She's not coming out," he said.

Her jaw dropped. "What's wrong with her? Is she sick?"

Travis shook his head. "She said she doesn't want to visit with you. She said she doesn't want to talk. She said...she said for you to go away."

The phone dropped from her hand and she hastened to pick it up, plastering it hard against her ear. "That's not possible. I need to see her. I *have* to talk to her. Please."

Travis's sympathetic look turned pitying. "There's nothing I can do, Lacy. I can't make her talk to you."

Lacy nodded, swiping impatiently at tears. "Thank you," she whispered, not looking at him to see if he heard her or not. Her hand fumbled with the phone a few times before she finally found the cradle and hung it up.

She stumbled outside and sat hard on the curb. Nothing in life had prepared her for the pain of her grandmother's rejection. What possible reason could the older woman have for not wanting to meet with her? There was no reason unless she was actually guilty. But, no, Lacy would never believe that. It wasn't only improbable; it was impossible. Besides the fact that her grandmother was the sweetest woman on the planet, she had no motive. She hadn't even known the victim.

Maybe her grandmother was embarrassed. After all, she was a very proper and private person who always preferred to keep her troubles to herself. Maybe she felt like Lacy shouldn't have to deal with the situation.

Yes, that had to be it. Her grandmother was suffering from misplaced pride. Somehow Lacy would have to get a message to her, but how?

"What are you doing?"

She looked up to see Jason in full uniform, staring down at her. The sun was behind him, casting his face into shadows.

"I was trying to see my grandmother," she said. The memory of last night's almost kiss gave her a heightened awareness of him, but she begrudged that awareness. She didn't want to be attracted to Jason. She had no time or interest in romance right now.

"What did you say to Buzz?"

"What?" She frowned up at him, shading her eyes. "Who's Buzz?"

He pointed toward the jail. "He answers the door."

"I thought his name was Travis."

"It is. We call him buzz because he buzzes people in. What did you do to him?"

"What are you talking about?" she asked, impatience creeping into her tone.

"He wants to ask you out. He hasn't stopped talking about you. He asked me if we were an item." Then, crossing his arms over his chest, he frowned down at her. "Look, Lacy, I don't know what you've been telling people about us, but I think maybe last night gave you the wrong idea. I'm not interested in a relationship."

She shot to her feet and brushed the dirt off her behind. "Are you out of your mind?" she practically shouted. "I don't know that guy." She jabbed a finger toward the jail. "He looks like a teenager; he must be a good six years younger than me. And as for you," she paused to jab her finger in his chest, wincing when it met with his rock-hard bullet-proof vest, "I have no interest in you, either. You have always thought that every girl in the room adored you, but you have always been wrong about me. I didn't want you in high school, and I don't want you now. I don't want anyone. The only thing I want is to clear my grandmother's name, get her out of jail, and move far, far away where cops don't arrest innocent old ladies and high school has-beens don't think the world of themselves."

To her chagrin, he laughed at her. "I have news for you: high school has-beens always think the world of themselves. That's universal. Just like the fact that redheads always have fiery tempers." He reached out to flick an end piece of her hair, but she batted his hand away.

"My hair is not red. It's strawberry blond. And don't touch me." She spun on her heel and stalked away from him.

"That's not what you said last night," he said, loudly enough for a group of people on the sidewalk to turn and look at them. She kept going. She wasn't sure she had ever been angrier or more mortified. By the time she slammed into her car and put on her sunglasses, he was gone. She rolled down the window and sat a few minutes, trying to simultaneously calm down and think of her next move.

Just as her brain was starting to clear, an answer appeared before her. Travis, or "Buzz," as Jason had called him, walked out of the building and toward his car. Could it be his lunch break already?

She stuck her head out of the window and called to him.

He paused and turned to look at her with a dawning smile of recognition. Throwing his hand in the air, he waved it back and forth. "Hi, Lacy."

She stepped out of the car and returned his wave. "Hi, Travis. Or do you prefer Buzz?"

He shrugged. "Whatever."

"Where are you off to?"

"I'm on a lunch run. I usually volunteer to pick up the food; it's a good way to get out of the office."

"Can I give you a ride?" she asked, leaning casually against her grandmother's Buick.

"I don't know. I saw you and Jason together last night." He glanced over his shoulder uncertainly. Was he looking for Jason?

"Jason and I went to high school together, that's all. How could I be interested in someone who arrested my grandmother?" *How, indeed?*

Travis turned back to her with a smile. "All right." With a shrug, he climbed into the passenger side of the Buick and buckled his seatbelt.

"Where to?"

"The taco place," he said.

"Can I ask you a question, Travis?" she asked. She darted him a glance before turning her attention to the road.

"What?" he asked. His tone was wary.

"How old are you?"

He smiled and relaxed into the chair. He was tall; much taller than Lacy's five feet and two inches. Even though the seat was pushed back as far as it could go, he still appeared folded in half. "Twenty one. How old are you?"

"Twenty five."

"You look younger," he said.

"So do you," she said. He laughed.

"I knew your sister," he said.

Her hands gripped the steering wheel tighter. "Hmm."

"Where is she now?"

"New York," Lacy said. The words left a bitter, acrid taste on the back of her tongue.

"That suits her," Travis said. "Riley was a year ahead of me, but she was one of those girls you knew was destined for greater things."

"Hmm," Lacy repeated. Blessedly, they arrived at the taco place and placed an order. As they waited for their food to be handed through the window, Lacy screwed up her courage. "Travis, what do they have on my grandmother?"

"Oh, I'm not, I mean, it's not really…Didn't Jason tell you?"

"Jason said he's a peon who doesn't handle investigations," she hedged.

42

"Jason lied. He's next in line for a promotion. Everyone knows when Brenner retires Jason's going to be the next detective."

"Are you going to get out of the jail and go on patrol?" she asked.

He shrugged. "That doesn't appeal to me so much. I think I'm a lifer in the jail." He sagged in his chair, staring dejectedly out of the window. It must be hard for a man to realize he wasn't cut out for a dangerous lifestyle, she thought.

"Doesn't the jail have a sergeant?" she asked.

"Yes," he said.

"You could be the jail sergeant. You would be good at it."

He perked up. "You think so?"

"I do. You're efficient and compassionate; that's a rare combination."

He turned to stare out the side window, a thoughtful expression on his face. "It was the pie."

"Excuse me?" she said.

"The pie. They found your grandmother's prints on a banana cream pie, and a witness placed her at the scene."

Lacy felt like all the air had been sucked from the car. Yesterday morning before she left, her grandmother had been baking a banana cream pie. Since she was always baking something, Lacy assumed it was for a funeral. "Why would the presence of a pie be enough for an arrest?"

Travis turned toward her again. "There were two pie plates and a knife. The woman was stabbed, and there were pieces of banana and whipped cream around the wound. A couple of witnesses saw your grandma deliver the pie and go inside. A few hours later, the woman was found dead."

"But dropping off a pie is a friendly gesture. Why would anyone drop off a pie, stay to eat, and then kill the person? That doesn't make any sense." She faced forward, drumming her fingers on the steering wheel.

"I'm going to tell you something about Detective Brenner," Travis said. "Something off the record: he's a lazy jerk. He jumps to the most obvious conclusion and then does as little work as possible to make the evidence fit his foregone conclusion. The situation is bad for your grandma, Lacy. The best advice I can give you is to hire a good lawyer. Maybe that Ed McNeil guy. He's smarmy, but he gets the job done."

Lacy's nose wrinkled in distaste at the dreaded name. "I'll think about it." Their order came up. She grabbed the bag and handed it to Travis. They were silent on the short drive back to the jail, but when they pulled into the lot he made no move to get out.

"Thanks, Travis. It was really nice of you to give me that information. I'm going to do my best to clear my grandma, and every little bit helps."

He smiled sheepishly, blushing faintly at the compliment. She blinked at him in surprise. He was no Jason, but he was cute. How was it possible that she, ordinary Lacy Steele, had made a guy blush?

"Lacy, I know you're sort of swamped right now, but maybe when this blows over we could go out sometime?"

"Thanks for the offer, Travis, but I just got out of a really serious relationship. I'm not ready to date again. And, to be honest, you're a little young for me."

"Four years isn't so much," he said.

"It is when I feel like I'm ninety. The last few years haven't been the best of my life. But I'm always looking for a friend." She smiled to gentle her rejection.

He smiled in return. "Maybe you'd better tell Jason you're not interested. He's staring at us through the patrol room window."

She fought the urge to turn and look. "What's he doing here, anyway? He doesn't usually come in until noon." She tried to subdue her own blush at the realization that she had Jason's schedule memorized.

"He's working overtime." Travis opened the door and stepped out. "See you Lacy."

44

"See you, Travis," she said. She waited until he closed the door and stepped onto the curb before she allowed herself to look toward the patrol room. She couldn't see Jason, but she did see the rustling of the mini blinds as they settled back into place.

Chapter 6

Six hours later, Lacy arrived home exhausted and drained. She had spent the afternoon interviewing Barbara Blake's neighbors as well as her grandmother's group of friends. Then she called and harassed Detective Brenner's secretary until she put her through to the detective. He had been surly and hateful, giving her only the sketchiest of details in the case, but it had been enough for Lacy to write the story for the paper and make her three o'clock deadline.

In the end, she had cobbled together enough facts to make a decent story. Len, the newspaper editor, had been duly impressed with her work and offered to call her whenever a story popped up. At any other time, Lacy would have been pleased to have located another source of income, no matter how small. But not now. Now she was frustrated and disappointed. While Lacy had established the rough facts of Barbara Blake's life and death, she hadn't found anything that would establish a connection between the deceased woman and her grandmother. She also hadn't uncovered a motive for the murder or any other suspects.

The remainder of her grandmother's friends protested her incarceration and repeated the same things that Gladys had told Lacy early that morning. Barbara had been a horrible woman. None of them had seen her since high school, and they were all certain there was no connection between her and Lucinda Craig, Lacy's grandmother. But, like Gladys, all of them had been cagey and nervous. And their stories were so similar that Lacy had the vague impression that they were rehearsed.

Nothing made sense to Lacy, and there was such a lag in information that there was no possible way to make sense of the few facts she possessed. For tonight she wanted nothing more than to go for a run, take a shower, then crash in her soft warm bed and lose herself in the oblivion of sleep.

Unfortunately, that wasn't to be. As soon as she pulled into her driveway, she noticed a man standing on the front porch. At first her traitorous heart began to thump hard in anticipation. Jason? Had he come to make amends? But, no, it wasn't Jason. This man was taller and his hair was lighter and longer. Then it hit her. She knew who he was, and she knew why he was here.

He turned to her with a smile as she slammed out of her car and bounded up the steps. He opened his mouth to speak, but she held up a hand to cut him off. "You can tell your boss that I don't want to hire him. If he were the last lawyer on the planet, I would rot in prison. Don't call here again. Don't step foot on my property. In fact, don't even look at me. I'm going to go inside and if you're still here in thirty seconds, I am calling the police to have you forcibly removed." By the time she finished her speech, she was practically panting with anger. It had felt a little too good to unleash her fury on this unsuspecting stranger, but at least she had made her point. Hopefully.

He smiled. She geared up to yell at him again, but this time he was the one who held up his hand to halt her. "I should really wear this when I make calls," he said. Reaching into his pocket, he pulled out a clerical collar and secured it over his polo shirt. She stared at it, dumbfounded.

"Please tell me this is some sort of ambulance-chasing lawyer trick to try and make me feel like a heel."

"No, sorry. It's a pastor's trick to try and make you feel like a heel." His smile widened and he held out his hand to her. "I'm the new pastor at your grandmother's church. I heard about her, uh, predicament, and came to offer my assistance."

Lacy put her hand in his while he pumped it a few times. "I don't even know where to begin. Is it a sin to yell at a preacher?"

"Depends on what you yell," he said. "I don't think you crossed any lines of eternal damnation, though. It sounds like you've had a bad day."

She shook her head. "Oh, no. Don't be nice to me now. Please, please, please be an obnoxious jerk so I can feel somewhat vindicated for yelling at you." She paused and bit her lip. "I don't suppose you ran over a puppy on your way over here, or did anything else heinous enough to deserve what I just vented on you."

He shook his head, his expression somber. "I rescued a kitten from a burning building and bought out a lemonade stand to send an underprivileged child to camp."

"Now you're just being cruel," she said.

He grinned at her and she realized he was still holding her hand. "Let me make it up to you; let's go grab something to eat."

She stared up at him, realizing he was very tall and lanky. His hair was brown and slightly shaggy as if he were a couple of weeks overdue for a trim. His eyes were brown and kind. All in all he resembled a puppy--playful and sweet.

Mistaking her inspection for reticence, he hurried on, "Think of it this way: I'm a pastor, and you need to talk. Plus, I'm new in town and hungry. You'd be doing me a favor."

"Okay," she agreed, wondering if she was crazy for agreeing to have dinner with a total stranger. Still, he had the kind of warm brown eyes that drew people in and made him seem trustworthy. "Where do you want to go? I'll meet you there." At least she wouldn't make the mistake of riding in a car with him.

"You choose. I've only been in town three days."

"The diner. Have you seen it? It's right off the highway on the edge of town."

He nodded. "I passed it on my way in, but I'll follow you in case I get lost." He stood aside, waiting for her to pass by him.

She did, and then threw him one more searching look over her shoulder. Why was she doing this? It was unlike her to make up to someone so easily, especially someone who had just been witness to an embarrassing meltdown. Was she really so lonely?

He smiled at her, and she had her answer. Yes, she was lonely, and tired, and stressed; she just wanted to spend the evening

48

somewhere other than her grandmother's lonely kitchen doing something other than eating leftovers and feeling sorry for herself.

The drive to the restaurant was blessedly short, not allowing her the opportunity to change her mind. Although she'd had enough time to become nervous. What would she talk to this man about? How did she look after a day spent chasing down dead ends?

A quick look in the mirror told her the result of her day wasn't good. The outside humidity had caused her hair to frizz around her face, and what few traces of makeup she'd applied than morning had already melted off. She parked in the first available spot and ran a brush through her hair a few times, touched up her eye makeup, and blotted her sweaty face with some translucent powder. It wasn't great, but it was a vast improvement so that by the time she met the guy at the door, she felt somewhat presentable.

"I just realized I don't know your name," she blurted.

Before he could answer, a hostess greeted them and led them to a conspicuous table in the center of the crowded restaurant. Lacy wanted to crawl under the table when she felt every eye turning to look at them. She knew many of the people who were looking at her, if not by name then by reputation. To make matters worse, many of them attended her grandmother's church. What would they say when they learned the mystery man she was dining with was their new pastor?

She licked her lips and gave a nervous glance toward the door. The last thing she wanted was to become the center of gossip. Was it too late to make a break for it?

"Tosh."

She turned to stare at the preacher, looking up to do so. "Excuse me?"

"You asked me my name. It's Tosh." He indicated her chair with a wave of his hand, and waited until she sat before taking his own chair.

"I've never heard that name before."

He smiled as he picked up a menu. "Apparently labor was pretty awful when I was born. My mom was so relieved to have medicine that she promised to name me after the anesthesiologist. Unfortunately for me, she was a woman named Natasha."

Lacy's eyebrows rose. "Your name is Natasha?"

He shook his head. "My mother is the type of person who sticks to her word, no matter what. She regretted her pain-induced vow, but she didn't feel right about going back on it, even though the doctor in question probably couldn't have cared less. Instead she changed the name slightly. Instead of Natasha, it's just Tosh."

"What's your last name?" she asked.

"Underwood."

"That's almost as bad as my name," she said sympathetically.

"What's your name?"

"Lacy Steele."

"What's wrong with that? It's pretty; it suits you."

"I've always hated it. It's an homage to my grandmother, I guess. Her name is Lucinda, though only her closest friends call her Lucy."

He put down his menu and put on what she guessed was his official pastor's face. Somehow he managed to look concerned and wise at the same time, which was a feat because he was very young.

"I heard she was arrested yesterday for murder."

"She didn't do it," Lacy said defensively. "She's the sweetest person in the world. And besides that, there's no motive and very little evidence."

His expression slid into a perplexed frown. "No offense, but that's an odd thing to say. What would you know about motives and evidence? Are you in law enforcement?"

"No. I'm a writer. I spent the day tracking down leads."

He leaned in and rested his face in his hand. "Did you find anything?"

She shook her head just as the waitress arrived, delaying any further conversation. Lacy ordered and watched while Tosh made

50

easy, polite conversation with the waitress. She had never been one of those people for whom social interaction came easily, and she was amazed by his gift of gab.

"You're staring at me," he said when the waitress walked away.

"Do they teach you how to talk to people at pastor school?"

"No. They tried to teach me how *not* to talk to people. I have the unfortunate habit of blurting out the first thing that pops into my head without running it through a filter first--not good for the politicking required of pastors today."

"Politicking?" she echoed.

"Being a pastor is a little like being elected to public office. You have to make your board and your parishioners happy while still fulfilling your calling to preach. It takes a finesse that I'm afraid I haven't developed yet."

"You seem good at it to me."

"That's because you've only seen me in happy situations. I have no tolerance for hypocrisy or meanness within the church. I'm afraid I'm a little too good at speaking my mind."

"Is that why you're here in my grandmother's tiny church instead of somewhere bigger?"

"That's one of the reasons," he said. "Another is because I'm young and this is my first senior pastorate. Also, I wanted to come here. I grew up in Chicago. I've always wanted to live in a small city."

"Are you crazy? Small cities are the worst." Realizing how loudly she blurted that last sentence, she leaned forward and lowered her voice. "Everyone knows everyone else's business and there's nothing to do. We don't even have any decent restaurants." She said the last statement just as the waitress arrived with their food. It wasn't her imagination that her plate landed in front of her with a slight thump.

When the waitress walked away, she realized Tosh was trying not to laugh.

"This is really not my day," she told him.

"If you hate it here so much, why don't you get out?"

"I did for a while. Turns out the big city wasn't so great, either. Maybe there's nowhere for me." She knew how pathetic she sounded, but she couldn't help it. Right now she was at the end of her emotional tether.

"What happened?" Tosh asked.

She picked up her fork and cut her chicken, not sure if she wanted to answer.

"Sorry, I'm also intensely nosy," Tosh explained. "You don't have to tell me if you don't want."

Suddenly she found that she did want to tell him, though she had no idea why. She was generally a private person. "I went to New York right out of college. I had a job. It paid well, but not well enough to afford Manhattan. I had a few roommates and we found a slum uptown. Everything was going great. To date, it was the best time of my life."

"I sense a 'but' coming," he interrupted.

She shook her head. "Not for a while yet. The only thing missing was a guy, but I didn't really mind. I've never been the type of girl who needs to be dating someone. And then I met Robert. He was charming. I know that's an old-fashioned word, but it's the best description I can think of. He was just so charismatic that everyone was drawn to him, myself included. Amazingly, the attraction was mutual, and we started dating almost from my first week at my new job. A year and a half later we were engaged."

She paused and looked down at her chicken a moment before continuing.

"Next comes that 'but' we spoke of," she began again. "A few months ago, my little sister, Riley, came for a visit. Apparently Robert and love at first sight are great friends because it happened again with her. While I was working, they were making plans behind my back. Robert dumped me and now he and Riley are together. We were only a few months from our wedding. I had to cancel everything." She paused again, swallowing hard. "I couldn't stay there

52

after that. Robert and I worked in the same office. I couldn't see him day after day, knowing…"

She looked down in surprise when he covered her hand on the table. "I'm sorry," he said gently.

Something inside her shifted slightly with that soothing gesture. A little of the tightness in her chest eased. Just knowing that someone somewhere cared and understood was like a healing balm. Her family was torn between wanting to support her and not wanting to condemn Riley. But Tosh didn't have the moral dilemma of having to choose between two sisters. He was fully on her side, and he cared about her pain.

Embarrassing tears stung her eyes, but they dried quickly when someone spoke beside her.

"Is this your boyfriend?"

Chapter 7

Jason towered over them, his dark uniform making him seem even more intimidating. Tosh let go of Lacy's hand and sat back, studying the newcomer as Jason studied him.

"What are you doing here?" Lacy asked Jason, catching his attention so he turned from Tosh to her.

"They have good coffee here," he explained. "I'm on a break." The way he looked at her was…odd. Was there accusation in his expression before he looked back to Tosh and held out his hand. "Jason Cantor."

"Tosh Underwood," Tosh replied, shaking Jason's hand.

"Jason and I went to high school together," Lacy explained to Tosh. Turning to Jason, she tried hard to keep her tone neutral. "Tosh is the new pastor at my grandmother's church."

Jason's eyebrow rose. "You look young to be a pastor."

"You look young to be a cop," Tosh returned.

Lacy frowned slightly as she looked between them. There were undercurrents she didn't understand. Were they sizing each other up, or was it her overactive imagination? But why would they? Jason had made it clear he wasn't interested, and she had known Tosh for less than an hour.

"I should get back to it," Jason said. "Nice meeting you." Turning to Lacy, he paused and tipped his head. "Stay out of trouble, Lacy."

She scowled at him. "When have I ever been in trouble, Jason?"

He shrugged. "Just be careful."

Her frown followed him as he walked away.

"Did you guys date in high school?" Tosh asked.

"No. We've never dated. We barely even know each other."

"Hmm," Tosh said. "Interesting."

"Why is that interesting?"

He shrugged. "It just is. So tell me about your grandmother. What happened?"

She set down her fork and launched into the story of her grandmother's shocking and bizarre arrest.

"So this detective thinks she did it, even though he only possesses the sketchiest of evidence," Tosh said.

"Yes," Lacy returned, her anger at the overbearing Detective Brenner bubbling to the surface once again.

"And your grandmother's group of friends insists your grandmother didn't do it, but they're also acting suspiciously."

"Yes," Lacy agreed. It was nice to have a sounding board to unload her worries on.

"And your grandmother refused to see you," Tosh said.

"Yes." Lacy's voice wobbled a little then.

Tosh gave her a sympathetic smile. "So what's your next move?"

The waitress returned to the table with their check before Lacy could answer. Tosh waved away her offer to pay, insisting that he would pay since he was the one who asked. He took their bill to the register and paid while Lacy trailed behind him, feeling helpless and flustered. If he asked her out and paid, did that make this a date? If so, how had she found herself on a date with a stranger?

"I'm going to follow you home to make sure you get there safely," Tosh said. "My mother would kill me if I didn't," he added when Lacy opened her mouth to protest.

Her house was only a few blocks away, so the drive was very short. He walked her to the porch and leaned against the wall, crossing his arms over his chest in a casual position. "Before we were interrupted at the restaurant, you were telling me what you plan to do next to help your grandmother."

She smiled at him, inordinately pleased that he was such a good listener and seemingly so interested in her mundane life. She glanced around, wetting her lips with her tongue, trying to decide if she trusted him. Oddly, she realized she did. Maybe it was his

55

unassuming manner, or maybe it was the fact that he was a pastor. Whatever the reason, she found herself leaning in to whisper.

"I'm going to search the dead woman's house."

Tosh looked down at her, his mouth slightly agape with surprise. "Do you have permission to do that?"

She shook her head.

"Isn't that sort of dangerous and against the law?"

Suddenly she realized she had just confessed her plan to do something illegal to her grandmother's new pastor. Was he honor-bound to report her to the police? He smiled as if reading her thoughts.

"Won't your policeman friend frown on that sort of behavior?" he asked.

Her eyes narrowed and she leaned against the doorframe, mimicking his pose. "What he doesn't know won't hurt him. Jason and I don't agree on much."

"Still, that seems risky." He bit his lip and looked away. "I wish I could go with you and be a lookout."

She was so surprised she laughed out loud.

He grinned down at her. "What? You don't think pastors ever want to do something crazy and adventurous? But it probably wouldn't do for my first official act here to be breaking into a dead woman's house."

"No, it wouldn't do at all," she agreed.

He reached out and touched his index finger to her hand. "Be careful."

She looked at his hand touching hers and felt her cheeks heat with a blush. "I will."

He stood straight and so did she. "I should go. I have a full day of meeting my new flock tomorrow."

She nodded as if she had any concept of what that meant. To her a day spent meeting strangers sounded like a punishment. "Thanks for supper," she said.

56

"No, thank you," he said. With a secret smile she didn't understand, he turned and walked away.

She stayed on the porch until his car was out of sight, then she let herself in and changed her clothes. After living in New York for three years, she had no shortage of black clothing. She sifted her grandmother's junk drawer until she located a flashlight, and then she was on her way. The last rays of the sun were just beginning to descend and it was still light outside, so she pretended she was a jogger out for her evening run.

Ten minutes later, she jogged past Barbara Blake's house. It looked exactly as it had when she saw it this afternoon- dark and uninhabited. Lacy jogged to the end of the street and stopped, pretending to bend over and check her shoelace. In reality she was surveying the neighborhood.

From the small, well-kept houses, she guessed the neighborhood to be full of elderly inhabitants. For her part, that was a very good thing. If her grandmother was any example, older people tended to turn in early and rise almost as soon as the sun was up. That meant that many of the people in this neighborhood were either already in bed or headed there. As if to prove her theory, many of the houses were darkened or had a light only in what appeared to be a bedroom.

There were a few houses with lighted living rooms, but none was close to Barbara Blake's house.

The street was a cul-de-sac, and for that Lacy was thankful. The end of the street behind her was a wooded area. She slowly inched backwards until she faded into the woods, and then she wove sideways until she was parallel with Ms. Blake's back yard. She had only to creep through two yards until she reached the house in question. Neither house was lit, but Lacy still felt like people were watching her as she darted around any object she could find, stealthily making her way toward her target.

Not until she reached the back porch did she remember the front door had been the one that was unlocked. But, to her great relief, when she tested the back door, it was also unfettered. She bit her lip as she soundlessly and slowly slid the door open, just wide enough to allow access. After slipping inside, she spent a moment allowing her eyes to adjust to the dim light. She had a flashlight but hoped to get by without using it.

The back door opened into the kitchen, so that was where she started her search. The room looked un-lived in, with only the barest of necessities such as a handful of plates and dishes. The drawers were mostly empty, making quick work of her search. The next room, the den, was much the same. The furniture was bare bones and dusty, requiring only a quick glance to sweep the entire room. After satisfying herself that there were no hidden closets, she quickly moved on. Next was a bedroom, and it was completely empty.

Just when Lacy was beginning to feel discouraged, she located the master bedroom--a sharp contrast to the rest of the house. This room was crowded with personal items, and it was clear that someone had been living here. Lacy's heart beat hard with anticipation as she began slowly sifting the contents of the room. There was no time to think about the fact that she was touching a dead woman's things. Instead, she focused on her task. She would deal with any ethical repercussions later.

The first thing she noticed was that Barbara Blake had expensive taste. Lacy didn't know much about the large pile of jewelry sitting on the dresser, but she thought some of it might be worth something. However, years of living in the fashion capitol of the United States had taught her a lot about labels. If the labels in Ms. Blake's closet were any indication, she was either very wealthy or had a very wealthy friend who kept her in finery. By Lacy's amateur calculation, the handful of clothes she looked at had to be worth at least twenty thousand, or maybe more. And that was without adding in the cost of the designer shoes that also lined the bottom of the closet. If Ms. Blake had no female relatives, then some thrift store was about to receive a bonanza.

Though her wardrobe was interesting, it wasn't what Lacy was looking for. Her heart sank as she finished her search and still hadn't found anything worthwhile to her cause. She was just about to walk out of the room when she remembered to check the most obvious hiding place in any bedroom.

Returning to the bed, she strained as she lifted the mattress and ran her hand underneath. She almost wanted to yelp with giddiness when her hand connected with something solid. After reaching in a little farther, she pulled out three hardbound books that looked suspiciously like journals.

Tucking them into the waistband of her pants, she finally left the room. The next door revealed a bathroom. Once again, Lacy was struck by the expense of the cosmetics and toiletries that lined the small room. Whatever the murderer's motive, it most likely hadn't been robbery unless they had no idea how much Parisian perfumes and designer clothes and shoes cost.

Lacy stopped short to think about that. Maybe someone who had such expensive taste in items also had piles of money sitting around somewhere. Maybe the murderer really had no idea how much the remaining items had cost and instead took whatever money he could find. Lacy made a mental note to try and find out something about the dead woman's financial situation.

After leaving the bathroom, only the living room remained to search. The sun had set too much to allow any remaining rays into the house. Lacy realized her mistake when she stepped into the room. She should have started her search here because it was on the front side of the house and had a large picture window in the middle of the room. Now she would be forced to use her flashlight, and there was a chance someone might see her.

Still, it had to be done. Just this one last room, and then she could leave. Even if someone called the police, chances were good that she could make a clean break before they arrived.

She pulled out her grandmother's flashlight, aimed it at the ground, and turned it on. And that's when a sound behind her sent a flood of adrenaline through her veins. Before she could turn and look, something hard and heavy connected with the back of her skull and she dropped to the ground, as lifeless as a stone.

Chapter 8

Jason Cantor slammed the door on his cruiser, causing his coffee to slosh over the side of his cup and burn his hand. He forced himself to take a deep breath and put the coffee in the holder before he could do something rash like hurl it at the opposing door.

Life wasn't going well lately. Instead of resting his head on the steering wheel like he wanted, he signed back on the air and started the car, wishing and hoping that for once something would be going on that demanded his complete attention. Not that things didn't go wrong in their small town. He knew better than anyone what secrets lurked behind closed doors. But lately he felt like his job was adding to his stress instead of taking away from it.

For all of his life, he had wanted to be a cop. His career was what he had prepared for and dreamed about. He could easily have gone to a bigger city where there was more crime, but it was important to him to remain in his hometown where he had the best chance of making a difference. But lately he was beginning to doubt that decision. More and more he felt like running away without ever looking back.

Day after day he went through the same mundane routine of delivering civil papers to divorcing spouses, handling landlord and tenant disputes, and calming parents who were arguing over custody arrangements. And when he wasn't doing any of that, he was sitting in the town's speed trap, handing out tickets. Since nothing was going on and since he didn't feel like driving around looking for trouble, he drove to the speed trap, turned on his radar, and sat behind the big billboard, halfheartedly wishing for someone to come along while at the same time wishing everyone would stay away.

He didn't like to give tickets. For him they meant only paperwork and arguments. True, some jerks deserved it. Some people drove so recklessly that they were a danger to others. But most of the people he ticketed were nice people barely pushing the bounds of the law. But, like everything else in his job, giving tickets was out of his control. His bosses had imposed a ticket quota on him, and if he didn't meet it each month he received discipline.

Consequently he spent his time preying on mostly innocent drivers who believed he was a typical small-town cop who loved nothing better than handing out speeding tickets, when in reality it was the part of his job he liked the least.

Well, almost the part he liked the least. The part he truly liked the least was standing by while the higher ups made stupid mistakes like arresting Lucinda Craig. If there was anyone less guilty of murder in the universe, Jason had yet to meet her. But what he had told Lacy was correct; he was a peon. Detective Brenner was a closed-minded jerk. If Jason had disagreed with him in any way, it would only have backfired and increased his bloodlust for the old woman. And the worst part was that Jason couldn't tell Lacy he agreed with her. Knowing her the way he was beginning to, she would use the information to go off half-cocked and do something crazy, something that would get both of them in trouble.

He smiled, thinking of Lacy. She was so unexpected that he still couldn't get over the shock of seeing her again. He would never forget that day a month ago when he had been walking down the street on one of his rare days off, minding his business, when a pretty redhead stepped out of the coffee shop and blinked up at the sun as if she were a mole seeing daylight for the first time. He had stopped short, realizing at once that she was new in town. He definitely would have remembered someone with curves like hers. With her long red-gold hair, grass green eyes and porcelain complexion, she was memorable, to say the least. She wasn't beautiful, exactly, but attractive and captivating in a way he didn't understand.

Then, and to his utter astonishment, she turned to look at him with recognition and he realized he *knew* her. Although he hadn't been able to summon her name at first, he instantly recalled the vision of her from high school. She had been one of the smart kids who played in the marching band and worked on the yearbook. Only at that time she had been chubby with frizzy red curls, glasses and braces.

They hadn't been friends in high school, but they hadn't been enemies, either. In fact, their two worlds hadn't intersected at all. Though they had gone to school with each other since kindergarten, they had never exchanged a word. So it was all the more amazing that he found himself angling toward her on the street that day, searching his brain for an opening line.

Since that time, he hadn't been able to get her off his mind. He had tried, without success, to learn as much as possible about her. He still had no idea why she had returned to their Podunk town after living in New York, but he sensed there was a story. There was something about her that seemed hurt or broken in some way, and he found to his chagrin that the more time passed the more he longed to know her, really know her.

But, try as he might, he couldn't gain a foothold with her. To say she was standoffish was putting it mildly. Oh, she watched him, but it was the same way an entomologist watches a fly, as if she were seeing something mildly interesting, but not interesting enough to tempt her. And that annoyed him--a whole lot.

He had dated a lot of girls and never once been rebuffed by someone he wanted. Although he knew it was a cliché, it annoyed him that Lacy seemed uninterested in him. Not that he wanted to date her. Despite his helpless attraction to her, he knew she wasn't for him. She was too high maintenance.

Not that she was clingy or needy--quite the opposite. Lacy was one of those girls who was so independent, self-sufficient, and unassuming that it would probably be the guy who found himself constantly pursuing her. Jason was chagrined to admit that he liked to be needed and wanted. Maybe it was because he was a cop and had a strong protective instinct. Whatever the reason, he wanted to be the solid one in a relationship. He wanted to be adored and fawned over. Lacy wasn't the fawning type. She was so proud and stubborn it would probably take a deathbed confession for her to ever admit to having feelings for anyone. And whatever had happened to her in New York had only worked to reinforce her protective shell. A guy would have to use a hammer and chisel to get at her heart again, and Jason just didn't want to have to work that hard.

But even though he knew they were all wrong for each other, he couldn't stop thinking about her. Lately he had taken to baiting her just to get a rise out of her. Early on after her return, he had learned that her ironclad self control slipped whenever she was angry. Since then, he found himself teasing her, testing her limits and then relishing the outcome whenever he succeeded in making her angry.

He smiled. Lately he had made her angry a lot, like last night when she called him a high school has been.

His smile slipped and his look became thoughtful as he ignored the cars speeding past him. Last night he had come so close to giving in and kissing her. If she knew how much self-control he was exerting in her presence, she might cut him some slack. But he was doing both of them a favor by keeping things light. They were all wrong for each other, and they both knew it. He was football and fried food; she was Jane Austen and sushi. Both of them were too strong-willed to ever give an inch on anything. No doubt once the initial physical attraction burned itself out, they would end up fighting all the time. Jason had no plans to live his life that way, ever. In fact, he pretty much planned to stay single for the remainder of his life. Being alone meant never getting hurt, never giving too much, never having too much taken away. Occasionally on holidays he felt glimmers of loneliness, but for the most part he was happy with his carefree life. He had no plans to let anyone ruin the good thing he had going, especially not a pretty little redhead with a volcanic temper.

But even though he didn't want to date her, he didn't want anyone else to date her, either. He was humiliated to realize he was jealous not only of Buzz, the jailer she had effortlessly charmed, but of the mystery guy from the restaurant.

64

Who was this new guy, Tosh? And if he was so new, how had he been able to gain a foothold into Lacy's life when Jason had been circling her for weeks without ever finding a crack in her defenses? His instincts went into overdrive imagining the worst about the newcomer. It was a felony to use law enforcement resources for personal motives, but Jason had never been more tempted to run a full background check on a non-criminal before.

Or maybe the man wasn't as innocent as he appeared. Wasn't it suspicious that this man arrived just when the town had its first murder in two decades? And how convenient that he should immediately hook up with their only suspect's granddaughter.

Jason's frown deepened to a scowl. Maybe he wouldn't use official channels to investigate the new guy, but he could still make some discreet inquiries. In a town like theirs, someone always knew something. It was all a matter of finding the right person with the right information, which was exactly what needed to happen with the murder case.

The problem was that Detective Brenner had stopped asking. He thought he had tied up his case in a nice little package, and he had no need to keep searching for the truth. Meanwhile a sweet old lady was rotting in jail and the real killer was going free.

Jason's frustration mounted again until it reached the boiling point. He was caught in the middle, wanting to do the job correctly, wanting to help Lacy, but unable to do a thing for fear of losing his job. Detective Brenner was second only to the sheriff in terms of power. When he said "jump," it was Jason's duty to say "how high." It had never been easy to suffer under such a bumbling, overbearing man, but now Jason was almost at his breaking point. Having to keep his comments to himself and arrest Lacy's grandmother had been close to the last straw. If something didn't happen soon to change the situation, he was going to have to start taking matters into his own hands, job or no job.

With thoughts of his job came renewed focus. He glanced at his radar just as a car blew by him. Pulling out, he ran the car's tags, realized he was pulling over a repeat offender with a suspended license, and smiled. *Sometimes it's fun to be the one who gives people what they deserve*, he thought as he turned on his siren and increased his speed.

As he approached the car, he saw a crack pipe on the front passenger seat. *This is my lucky night.* Sometimes, like now when criminals were painfully stupid, Jason felt like the good guy. The man behind the wheel was high out of his mind, driving on a suspended license, and creating a possibly lethal problem for the community. Jason was fulfilling his purpose of keeping the community safe by arresting this man, especially because after he secured him in the back of the cruiser he found a loaded gun in the glove compartment. Some nights were good; most were not.

When backup arrived from the state patrol, he left the trooper to deal with the tow truck while he took his prisoner to jail. The process of booking the inmate and writing his report not only kept him busy for an hour, but kept his mind too occupied to think of anything else, namely Lacy.

He whistled when he left the station for one final patrol of the town. The night was almost over, and it had been a good one. Thanks to him, there was one less menace on the streets, and he could sleep well tonight knowing he had done his job.

Just as he was about to call it a night, he drove past the murder house. Out of the corner of his eye, he thought he detected a flash of light. Knowing the state patrol was in the middle of a shift change, he decided to check into the situation a little more before he called them for backup. What if he was wrong? What if it was nothing? He would look like an idiot or, worse, he would look like a rookie.

He slid the car into neutral and turned it off, allowing it to glide to a stop some distance from the house. Since it was summer, there was still some light outside, but it was shadowy enough that his black uniform didn't stand out. Placing his hand on his large flashlight, he crept around the side of the house. Just as he reached the last set of bushes at the corner of the house, the door burst open and a blurry form ran outside.

"Stop, police." As was the law, Jason identified himself, but of course it had the opposite effect; the shadowy figure picked up the pace. Jason gave pursuit for a few houses before realizing he had lost his quarry. He stopped short, looking around the darkening neighborhood and feeling frustrated. How had he lost the person? Even though the suspect had a head start, Jason was a fast runner who should have easily been able to catch up. He wasn't even winded from his pursuit as he stood looking around the yard, perplexed. It was as if the person had disappeared into thin air. Usually when a suspect fled he was so intent on getting away that he crashed through anything in his path, leaving sights and sounds as a clear path for any pursuing officer. Not today, though. There were no footprints, no trampled vegetation, and no sounds save for the crickets and frogs chirping nearby.

After another few seconds of inspecting the blank landscape, Jason turned and went back to the murder house. At the very least he could see what had been disturbed before he secured the scene.

Almost as soon as he slid open the back patio door and stepped inside, the hairs on his arm stood at attention. Someone was in this house. Not only could he sense a presence, but he could hear someone breathing. The fact that they remained in one place, making no attempt to get away, was even more alarming. Were they lying in wait with a weapon?

He pulled out his gun and slid the safety off. Stealthily he crept toward the next room and toward the breathing sound, hoping no one could hear the sound of his heart thumping. He had drawn his weapon on suspects before, but he had never had to shoot anyone. Would today be the first time?

His gun preceded him around the corner as he slowly followed, sweeping the room with a glance. He frowned in consternation. There was someone in this room; he could hear them. But he couldn't see them. Were they hiding in a closet? He took a step and his foot connected with something solid, startling him so that he took his gun and drew a bead on at the body lying on the floor, preparing himself to shoot if the person sprang at him.

Then he felt the color drain from his face as his hand thumped listlessly to his side. For a second he remained staring in shock at the mass of red hair fanned out on the carpet, and then he put the safety on his gun, holstered it, and knelt beside the inert form of Lacy Steele.

Chapter 9

"Lacy."

Someone was calling her name. There was a part of her that wanted to go toward the sound and wake up, but another, stronger part of her warned her to stay unconscious. The voice sounded equally angry and concerned.

"Lacy, wake up."

Calloused hands passed over her forehead, pushing her hair out of her face and lightly scraping her smooth forehead with their roughness.

"Wake up so I can kill you," the voice said, and all at once it came back to her. Jason was here. He had found her in Barbara Blake's house, and he was angry. No doubt when she came to, he would arrest her.

She groaned, not only because her head was killing her, but also because she was afraid. She didn't want to go to jail. How would it look for her family if she and her grandmother were both incarcerated in the same facility?

"*Can* you wake up?" Now his voice began to sound frightened. "Maybe I should call an ambulance."

That did it. There was no way she was going to the hospital on top of everything else, namely because she had no health insurance. Her eyes popped open, and she stifled the urge to groan again. Jason was very close to her face and, as she had suspected, he looked very angry.

"I could have killed you," he growled.

"I think someone else already tried," she returned.

"Do you have any idea how close I came to shooting you? I had my gun aimed at your head, Lacy. If you had moved…" He broke off and glanced away. "What are you doing here? Please tell me someone kidnapped you and dumped your body inside this house."

"Um, sure, that's what happened," she said shakily as she tried to sit up.

He growled in frustration and pushed her back down. "Just lie still for a few minutes. You have a giant goose egg on the back of your head. It'll be a miracle if you don't have a concussion."

Gratefully, she sank back to the ground and closed her eyes. To her surprise, he began gently running his hand over her head in an almost motherly gesture. She resisted the urge to lean into his touch, realizing how badly she needed comfort and reassurance. Right now she wanted nothing more than for someone to hold her and tell her everything was going to be okay.

"What happened?" he asked after a couple minutes. "The truth."

"I came here to have a look around." She paused when he groaned. "Someone else was already here. They bashed me in the back of the head. I don't know what happened after that."

"I think that's about the time I arrived," Jason said. He reached for her hand and gripped it tightly. "Do you have any idea what might have happened if I hadn't shown up? Or, even worse, if the other person hadn't been here, and I had been the one to find you? I could have shot you, Lacy. I would have had my gun drawn as soon as I realized there was someone here. One wrong move and I would have killed you." He squeezed her hand until it became painful.

She opened her eyes and looked up at him. "That didn't happen."

"But it could have." His voice sounded oddly choked as if he couldn't stop the mental image of what might have been.

Reaching up, she lightly brushed his cheek with her fingers. He blinked at her in surprise, but he couldn't be as surprised as she was by the gesture. She wasn't usually one to make physical overtures of affection.

"Are you going to arrest me?" she asked.

"Breaking and entering is a crime," he answered.

70

"Technically I didn't break. The door was unlocked. I simply entered."

"Trespassing is still a crime."

"The woman who owns this house is dead. Who is going to press charges?"

His face darkened and his lips pressed together in a grim line. "Lacy, if you didn't have a head injury, I would shake you. What were you thinking? Even though you want to try and dance around the issue, you broke the law. Do you know what kind of position this puts me in?"

She let him stew in his anger for a minute before answering. "But, Jason, this proves my grandmother didn't do it. Why else would someone be in this house if not to cover his tracks? I have to clear her name because no one else is going to do it. You know your detective thinks the case is all wrapped up. I can't let my grandmother go to prison for something she didn't do."

"He's not my detective, and you can't go around breaking the law, putting yourself in harm's way in order to try and solve this case."

"If I don't, then who will?"

I will, he wanted to say, but he couldn't. His hands were tied. If he bucked the system and asserted her grandmother's innocence, he would be out of a job quicker than he could blink. His only chance of helping her was to remain where he was and work within the system.

He sighed and sank back slightly on his heels, realizing as he did so that he was still holding her hand, his thumb gliding gently up and down her palm. Her skin felt smooth and soft and he stifled the sudden urge to let his lips skim over her hand. Right now relief and worry were mixed together and so acute that if he gave in to his desire to press her hand to his lips, he was afraid he wouldn't be able to stop there. It would be just his luck to have the state patrol show up unannounced and find him making out with a suspect on the floor of a sealed house.

"If I let you go, you have to promise never to do anything like this again. If I catch you breaking the law again, I'm going to have to do something about it," he said, trying to sound stern despite the raging attraction to her that nearly diverted all other, more coherent thoughts. Even half-conscious and sprawled ungracefully on the floor she was pretty.

"I just wanted to have a look around," she said, sounding very much like a little girl who had been caught with her hand in the cookie jar.

He almost smiled at her pouty tone. He sort of liked her helpless and at his mercy, but he should have known it wouldn't last. Putting her hand on his shoulder for support, she forced herself to a sitting position. Then, after wincing a couple of times, she shakily stood to her feet. He stood along with her, ready to catch her if she fell over. After swaying gently a few times, she seemed to find her balance.

"I'll drive you home," he volunteered.

"It's okay, I walked here. I can walk back."

He released air through his teeth, forcing himself to remain patient. "Lacy, you are not walking home in the dark with a head injury. You're riding with me."

She wrinkled her nose at him. "I don't want to ride in a police cruiser like a criminal."

"You *are* a criminal," he reminded her.

"Not officially," she said.

He swiped his hand over his face, feeling suddenly exhausted. "Just get in the car before I carry you. I've been working for twelve hours, and I don't have the patience to deal with your issues tonight."

Her jaw dropped in an affronted expression, but he ignored her and took a step closer, herding her toward the door. She turned on her heel, swayed, regained her balance, and marched toward the door with her head held high, her long hair trailing indignantly behind her like the angry swish of a cat's tail.

72

He made a quick tour of the house, securing all the doors and windows that should have been secured earlier by the state's forensics team. It was unlike them to be so unprofessional as to leave a door unlocked, but Jason was too tired to think of such things now. He tucked the puzzle of the unlocked door away in the back of his mind for later inspection.

When he slid behind the wheel of his cruiser, he knew she was angry at him. She sat beside him in the front passenger seat with her arms crossed over her chest. It took exactly three minutes of silence before she rounded on him.

"What issues?" she asked.

"Huh?" he asked, sparing her a glance before turning back to the road.

"You said you didn't have patience to deal with my issues. What issues?"

He wanted to bite his tongue for his stupidity. Had he really said that out loud? "It was nothing. Just forget it."

"No, I think I want to know what you meant," she said. She turned to face him, leaning her back against the door.

Suddenly his own anger kicked into high gear. His emotions were already in overdrive after this exhausting day, and he found himself spoiling for a good fight. "Fine. You want to know what your issues are? I'll tell you. You're headstrong, stubborn, proud, and an emotional recluse. A guy would need dynamite and a blasting cap to chip away at the barriers you've put around yourself. You might as well wear a flashing sign that reads 'Stay Away.'"

They pulled up in front of her grandmother's house. He would have opened her car door for her, but she had already stepped out and slammed it behind her when he reached her.

He trudged behind her as she marched up the porch steps like a freight train, anger evident in every step. She reached to open the door, but he stopped her by laying his hand on her arm.

"Let me search the house before you go in," he said.

"No. Go away." She reached for the door again, but he put his arm around her waist and drew her back against his chest. He expected her to fight him, but she didn't. She remained stiff and unyielding, holding herself as far away from him as she could.

"Lacy, the person who attacked you might know who you are," he whispered. Their contorted position put his mouth very close to her ear. "He could be waiting in your house right now. I need to search the premises; let me do my job."

She didn't relax, but she didn't protest further. He let her go and she stepped away from him, still keeping her eyes trained toward the dark horizon.

He took her key, opened the door, drew his weapon, and walked inside. Although his first impression upon entering the house was that it was empty, he took his time making a detailed sweep, checking the basement and closets.

"It's all clear," he said when he stepped back onto the porch. Lacy remained silent, still looking away from him. He sighed. "Look, Lacy, I'm sorry. We've both had a lousy day. I didn't mean to unload on you."

She rounded on him then and he resisted the urge to take a step back from the cold fury in her green eyes. When she put her hands on her hips and advanced on him, he did step back until he butted against the front of the house. She kept coming until she was only a few inches away, and then she unleashed the full power of her rage.

"You think I have issues? Well maybe I do, but I have good reason for my issues. What reason do you have for your overpowering fear of commitment, Jason? Soon you're going to find yourself as a forty year old cliché--chasing younger girls and reliving your glory days while the rest of the world settles down to responsible adulthood. Why don't you take a look in the mirror before you start handing out insults to me? I may be an ice princess, but I have a good reason. You have always been the center of everything. Your life is perfect. What's your excuse for your

74

emotional barriers? Don't pretend you don't have them because I've seen them, and they're as solid as mine."

She stood in front of him, her hands on her hips, her chest heaving with anger, and her long hair streaming around her face in wild disarray. Her cheeks were flushed, she was frowning, and he was certain she had never looked more beautiful. Instead of feeling upset by her reprimand, he found himself forgetting everything they had just said to each other.

"You're right," he agreed. "We're both a mess." Tentatively, he reached out and put his hands on her waist. She gave him a wary, surprised look, but she didn't back away. Taking that as a sign of encouragement, he pulled her closer, reeling her in slowly like a fish until she was pressed solidly against him. "Do you think it's possible our combined issues cancel each other out?"

"No, I think we're a horrible combination." Her palms flattened against his chest as if she were going to push him away, but instead she circled his neck and clasped her hands behind his head, standing on her toes to move closer to him.

"So do I," he agreed. He closed his eyes and bent to kiss her when his lapel radio crackled to life.

"Unit five, checkup," the dispatcher said.

Jason froze. "What time is it?" He checked his watch without waiting for an answer. "I got off duty an hour ago. I was supposed to report to the station for shift change. I've got to go."

Slowly her eyes opened and she stared up at him, dazed. Was he saying he was leaving? Now? "You're going?"

He smiled and touched her cheek with his index finger. "I have to." He paused to speak into his radio, and then he turned to look at her again. "I could come back after I go to the station and retrieve my car." There was a question in his statement.

Thankfully some sanity was beginning to return to her overheated brain. "Thanks, but I'll be fine." She unclasped her arms and stepped back out of his embrace.

He almost shivered from the new chill in the atmosphere. He wanted to be angry with her for rebuffing him, but she was correct. Together, they were a horrible idea. Better to keep things at the level of friends, if they could even be considered that. After all, they had less than nothing in common. He straightened and moved away from the wall.

"See you around, Lacy. Stay out of trouble."

She put her hands on her hips once again and frowned as she watched him walk down the steps. "I never look for trouble," she called after him.

"And yet it has a way of finding you," he called over his shoulder. Then he got in his cruiser and drove away.

Chapter 10

Not until Lacy undressed for bed a few minutes later did she remember the journals she had slipped into her waistband. Jason's bullet-proof vest was undoubtedly the only thing that had kept him from noticing the journals when they shared their latest embarrassing embrace.

She pulled the journals from her waistband and smacked them on the kitchen counter, too angry even to look at them right now. *Issues.* Jason had accused her of having issues, and the most frustrating part of the whole thing was that he was correct. Of course she had issues, how could she not after her fiancé dumped her for her sister?

Robert had been her first love, her first everything. Before him she had barely dated, but with him she had let down her guard entirely, giving him her complete trust. And what had he done with that trust? Shredded it. How could she ever trust anyone again, especially someone like Jason who looked too good to be true, told her repeatedly he didn't want her, and alternately ran hot and cold?

Lacy slammed a few cupboards until she found her grandmother's pain reliever. Checking the date on the bottle, she realized it was like most of the medicine in the cupboard: outdated. Still, what was the harm in taking pain reliever that was too old? Her head was killing her and there was nothing else, so she popped a couple of pills and downed them with water straight from the faucet, not even bothering with a glass.

With that task completed, she returned her attention to her furious thoughts about Jason. Really, she was angrier with herself than with him. Of course he was going to toy with her; it was his nature to do so. The problem was her reaction to him. Why did it seem like whenever she was within a few feet of him she turned into the sort of simpering idiot she had always despised? While other girls allowed their hearts to rule their heads, Lacy had remained sensible, always following her head. Even with Robert she had first made a list of pros and cons before going out with him. Only when she deemed he was an adequate risk did she say yes to his request for a date.

But with Jason she completely lost her mind the minute she looked into his beautiful face. He smelled perfect. He looked perfect. The only problem was that he *wasn't* perfect. Far from it--he was a mess for myriad reasons that leapt to the surface of her brain whenever she thought of him. Whereas with Robert she had turned a blind eye to his faults and deluded herself into believing he was okay, she had no such difficulty seeing the reality of Jason. Like a cardboard cutout of a model, he was all looks and no substance. She would have an easier time making a list of his faults than his assets. There was no way she could delude herself into thinking he was perfect; he wasn't. And yet she couldn't seem to get enough of him.

She crawled into bed, placing the journals on the pillow beside her. Before she could open them, her thoughts turned suddenly to Tosh. How odd that she should trust him after just meeting him, but she did. She had probably shared more of herself with him tonight than she had anyone except her grandmother.

And that was her final thought until the sun filtered through her window the next morning. Lacy woke with a start and looked at the pillow beside her, breathing a sigh of relief when she saw the journals lying sedately on the pillow. How could she have fallen asleep when she her only purpose last night had been to read those journals?

Her stomach rumbled, further delaying her purpose as she rolled out of bed and trudged to the kitchen for some food. Her grandmother's prune cake greeted her, offering up familiar comfort. Lacy picked up a fork and dug in, not waiting to cut a piece and put it on a plate.

Only after her belly was uncomfortably full did she realize how much of the cake she had eaten. She groaned and shoved the half-empty cake pan away from her. Now she would have to run in order to try and circumvent the calorie overload she had just consumed.

She took her time changing into her workout clothes, willing her food to digest so she wouldn't get sick while she ran. If there was one thing she hated more than running, it was running on a full stomach. Just as she was about to leave her room, she turned and caught sight of the journals. Maybe Jason was making her paranoid, but she thought maybe she should hide them on the off chance that someone came looking for them. Her first instinct was to shove them under her mattress, but if she had thought to look there at Barbara Blake's house, someone would most likely think of searching for them in the same place here. Instead she searched her closet for a loose board she remembered from her youth.

A distant cousin had once shown her the hiding place, and they had spent a happy afternoon pretending to be spies, hiding secret messages in the small space. The boards were warped when Lacy tried to pry them up, forcing her to retrieve a hammer from the garage. After painstakingly pulling it up, she slipped the journals inside and pushed the board back into place.

"There," she said out loud, dusting her hands on her pants. With her task completed, she forced herself to leave the house and jog the circuitous three miles she had staked out during her first week in town. Ideally, running three miles four times a week was what Lacy needed to keep her figure in tact. Without giving up the foods that she loved, she would never be skinny. But she liked her body as it was. Her hourglass figure was shapely, but she firmly believed women were supposed to have curves.

As she let herself in, the phone started to ring. She paused in front of the answering machine, vowing to take a hammer to it if she heard Ed McNeil's voice once again.

"Lacy, it's Jason." His voice sounded groggy, as if he had just rolled out of bed and dialed. "I wanted to make sure you're okay. Last night was...intense. Catch you later."

Almost as soon as his message ended, the phone started to ring again. She lunged for it, fumbling it to her ear. "Hello," she blurted.

"Lacy, it's Tosh. I'm calling to make sure you're not in the slammer. How did last night go?"

"Not well," she said, sinking into a kitchen chair. "I got hit over the head and knocked out."

"Are you kidding me? You could have been killed."

"That's what Jason said."

"Jason," he repeated.

"He showed up right after I got knocked out."

"So he saved you," he said.

"I suppose," she drawled, not understanding his dry tone.

"Did you at least find anything helpful?"

"I found some journals," she said with no idea why she was sharing such vital information with a man who was, for all intents and purposes, a complete stranger.

Tosh whistled. "Nice. I was also calling with some potentially good news. Apparently the deceased was a longtime member of my new church. I've been asked to do the funeral. There's a viewing tonight, and the service is tomorrow. Maybe if you show up and circulate you might find out something useful."

"Tosh, that's brilliant," Lacy replied. "Thank you."

"I was also calling to ask a favor of you. As far as I can tell, you seem to be the person in town who knows the most about Barbara Blake. Since this is my first funeral, and since I've never met the woman, I was wondering if you might be able to meet with me and impart some information about her."

"I would be glad to, but I have to warn you: most of what I know is pretty bad."

"At this point anything is better than the nothing I have. I'll do my best to put a positive spin on things. Can you do supper again?"

"Okay," she stammered, not sure how she found herself going out with this newcomer for a second night in a row.

"Great. We'll have to eat early and quickly because the viewing starts at six."

"No problem," she assured him. "I'm skipping lunch today. I just ate my body weight in cake."

"That sounds good," he said.

"I'll bring you some. I need to get it out of the house."

"Awesome. Later, Lacy."

"Later, Tosh." She hung up and stared at the phone so that she startled when it rang almost immediately.

"Hello," *Grand Central Station,* she added mentally.

"Lacy, it's Travis from the jail. Is this a bad time?"

"No, not at all." *Apparently this is my morning to receive gentleman callers.* "How are you?" She bit her lip, hoping he wasn't calling to ask her out again. She didn't want to have to reject him again.

"I'm good, and I have some good news for you. I spent a long time talking to your grandmother yesterday. She's agreed to see you this morning during visiting hours."

Lacy sat up, gripping the phone tightly to her ear. "Travis, that's amazing. How did you convince her?"

"I may have embellished your emotional state a little bit. It might be a good idea to work up a few tears before you see her," he suggested.

The back of her head throbbed, and she winced as tears of pain filled her eyes. ."I don't think that will be a problem. Travis, how can I ever thank you for this? This is possibly one of the sweetest things anyone has ever done for me."

"I can think of one way," Travis said. There was a breathless pause while she waited for him to continue. "Pick me up a coffee on your way in. I'm working overtime, and I'm zonked."

She smiled and relaxed. "Sure thing. I'll see you at ten. And, Travis, thank you."

"No problem, Lacy. See you later."

They disconnected, and Lacy sat back, feeling a bit overwhelmed. Three phone calls from three different men in the space of thirty minutes was definitely not a part of her normal routine. Maybe there was something to be said for living in a small town. Here she was a big fish in a little pond, and it was apparently mating season.

Her nose wrinkled at the unbidden imagery her thought created. "Gross," she murmured. Dispelling all thoughts of fish from her mind, she walked to the bathroom and took a lengthy shower.

A half hour later she was prepared to emerge from the house, clean, refreshed, and ready to start her day. She had even listened to the weather forecast, found out it was supposed to be humid, and secured her hair in a braid down her back. People with wavy strawberry-blond hair know better than to let their hair have free reign on humid days. If she let her hair have its way, by noon she would be able to try out for the starring role in *Annie*. She opened the door and swallowed a yelp of surprise when she ran into a solid form on the front porch.

"You didn't answer your phone," Jason said accusingly. He was scowling at her, but it was difficult to take him seriously when his lustrous black hair stuck up in patches all over his head. Apparently she wasn't the only one with hair humidity issues.

"I didn't know your hair was naturally curly," she blurted, staring at his head.

He used his hand to try and tame his locks to no avail. "I haven't showered yet. I just woke up and had a mini panic attack, wondering if you made it through the night. How's the head?" Now it was his turn to stare at her hair. "Nice braid."

Since she wasn't sure if the compliment was sincere or sarcastic, she ignored it. "It hurts, but I took some pain reliever from the eighties, so it should start feeling better any minute now."

"Huh?"

"Never mind."

As they stood on the porch inspecting each other, an awkward silence descended between them. "Have you eaten?" she asked for lack of something better to say.

"Since I rolled out of bed, called you, and then hopped in my car, you mean? The answer is no," he said grumpily.

She turned and led the way back inside. "Come on. Sit down." She pointed toward the kitchen table. "Do you like prune cake?"

His lip curled. "I don't know. It sounds awful."

Offended by his mockery of her favorite food, she retrieved a clean fork from the drawer, scooped a bite of cake onto it, and shoved the whole thing in his mouth. He grabbed her hand and plucked the fork from it, but dutifully chewed and swallowed the cake.

"All right, that's pretty good," he admitted. "But I can't just eat sugar for breakfast. Do you have any eggs?"

"Are you actually suggesting that I cook for you?" she asked.

"After I drove all the way over here to check on you? You'd better believe it." He leaned back and grinned at her, lacing his fingers behind his head and propping his feet out in front of him.

She stared at him, trying to decide if she was going to refuse his request, but the longer she gazed at him, the better he looked. After a few beats, she gave up, turned toward the fridge, and retrieved the eggs.

"Do you have any coffee?" he asked.

"I usually get my coffee from the café," she said.

"Does that mean you don't have any?"

"I do have coffee, but I don't know how to make it," she admitted sheepishly. Since her freshman year of college, she had always bought coffee already made by someone else.

Jason stood and shuffled to the counter where he began opening cupboards until he located the coffee. "C'mere," he said, grabbing her wrist and pulling her toward him. "The water goes here." He poured water into the back of the pot. "Then you put in a filter and add coffee--one tablespoon for every two cups. I'm making eight cups, so that's four tablespoons of coffee. Close this, push the button, and that's it."

If his tone had been condescending, she would have come back with a sarcastic reply. Instead he had spoken sincerely and patiently. "That doesn't look so hard," she said meekly.

He smiled at her and glanced at the eggs. "Do you know how to make eggs, or should I do those, too?" There was the condescension that had been missing from the coffee lecture.

"Sit." She shoved at his chest. "I can make eggs. I can make many things. My grandma taught me to cook and bake."

"But not to make coffee," he said.

"She doesn't drink it since my grandfather died, and I was too embarrassed to ask for a lesson. It's such a simple thing; I should already have known how to do it."

"Now you know," he said. He resumed his seat at the kitchen table and watched her while she deftly cracked a few eggs into a bowl and stirred them with a whisk. She didn't ask him how many he wanted, instinctively knowing that three was the correct number. He smiled when her whole body wiggled as she used the whisk. "I like my eggs well beaten," he said when she put down the whisk.

She paused to look at him over her shoulder. "Weird," she muttered, then she picked up the whisk and resumed stirring. After another minute, she turned to look at him again. "Is that enough whisking?"

"For now," he said, smiling wider when she gave him a look that told him she thought he was crazy.

He continued to study her as she devoted herself to the eggs, turning them, salting them, and then removing them from the heat at just the right moment as if she knew he liked his eggs slightly moist. She slid them onto a plate, added a generous serving of prune cake, poured him a cup of coffee, and set both plate and cup before him.

"Thanks," he said, trying to remember the last time a girl had cooked for him.

84

She smiled and sat at the table beside him.

"Aren't you eating?" he asked.

"I already ate."

"At least have a cup of coffee with me. I hate eating alone."

She smiled, remembering how he had insisted she order a soda the night he took her to makeout point. She stood again, poured herself a coffee, and sat, only then realizing that he had pulled her chair closer to his when her back was turned. She found it odd that a guy who valued his bachelorhood as if it were a priceless treasure seemingly hated to be alone.

"This coffee is actually good," she said as soon as she took a sip.

"You doubted me? By the way, the eggs are good, too."

"You doubted me?" she asked. He looked up and they shared a smile.

"What's on your agenda today?" he asked.

"I'm going to visit my grandma."

"Do you think she'll see you today?"

She nodded. "Travis convinced her."

His fork froze halfway to his face. "Buzz? What's between you two, anyway?"

"It's called friendship. You see, there are some people in the universe for whom platonic relationships come naturally. Not all of us have to date every available member of the opposite sex."

"Wow, breakfast and a lecture. It's like being at a conference," he said before shoving the forkful of egg into his waiting mouth. She nudged his leg with her foot and he caught it, settling it into his lap and resting his hand on her ankle. Lacy wasn't sure which of them looked more startled by his action. He cleared his throat and tried to ignore the new, intimate position he had created for them. "What else have you got going on today?"

She glanced at the far wall, wondering if she should tell him about the journals. Why was it so easy to tell Tosh about them and so difficult to tell Jason whom she had known all her life? "I'm going to Barbara Blake's viewing tonight."

"Are you sure that's a good idea?"

"Why wouldn't it be a good idea?" she asked.

"I don't know, maybe because there's a murderer out there who possibly tried to kill you last night," he retorted, shoveling in a fistful of eggs and chewing angrily.

She sat up and removed her foot from his lap. "So you admit you think my grandmother is innocent."

"Of course she's innocent," he practically yelled. "I've never believed otherwise."

"Then why did you arrest her? Why didn't you stand up for her from the beginning?"

He sat back and ran his hand through his hair. "You are just...How would it have helped you for me to get fired?"

"'All that is necessary for evil to triumph is for good men to do nothing,'" she quoted.

"That's a great quote, Lacy. I'm sure it would have kept me warm on the unemployment line."

"You don't know you'll get fired if you stand up for what's right. And even if you do, isn't doing the right thing worth anything you might suffer?" she asked.

"Where am I supposed to go if I lose my job? Not everyone has the luxury of a loving grandmother waiting to pick up the pieces of our broken lives. All I have is myself, and I have to do whatever it takes to take care of me. Ideals are great, but they don't pay the rent."

"You are just so..."

"What? Different from you? Are you so closed minded that you think everyone who doesn't agree with you is necessarily wrong? And, while we're on the subject, what is it you aren't telling me? What are you hiding from me, and don't say nothing because I can tell there's something." He studied her, noting the conflicting expression fleeting across her face. "Trust me." He leaned in and lowered his voice. "I'm a cop."

86

"It's because you're a cop that I can't trust you with this," she said.

He froze, turning the words over in his mind. "You found something in her house last night."

She bit her lip and nodded, her eyes rounded with worry over his reaction.

Nervously, he scraped his bottom teeth over his lip. He was walking a very fine line here. "What did you find?"

The pulse in her neck jumped. He stared at it, wanting to touch it, wanting to ease her anxiety. "Some journals," she said.

The news was worse than he thought. If the journals contained the identity of the killer, they would be inadmissible in court. Not only that, but if it somehow came to light that he had helped support an illegal search of the house and then suppressed evidence, he would not only lose his job, he would be prosecuted.

"Have you looked at them yet?" he asked.

"No," she whispered. Would he make her turn them over to the police, sight unseen?

"Go get them," he commanded.

Nervously, she scurried down the hall to her room. With shaking hands, she peeled up the floorboards and returned with the journals. She set them on the table between them and resumed her seat, sitting on her hands and resisting the urge to fidget.

While she was gone, Jason finished his food and poured himself another coffee. He also retrieved a clean cloth napkin from a drawer and used it to open one of the journals. Lacy's mouth went dry when she realized what he was doing; she hadn't even thought to protect the book from her fingerprints.

"Does any of this mean anything to you?" he asked.

He made room for her as she leaned in to look at the book. "It looks like some sort of code," she said.

"Hmm." They stared at the book together in silence awhile as she turned pages.

"Wait," she said. "There." She tapped a page in the book. "Jimmy Choo's. I saw a pair of Jimmy Choo's in her closet."

"I have no idea what that means," he said.

"They're shoes, very expensive shoes."

"How expensive?" he asked.

"The cheap ones start at around seven hundred."

His mouth fell and he shook his head. "Ridiculous," he muttered. "Do you see anything else you recognize?"

As a unit, they leaned closer to the book. She jumped and looked at him when he rested his hand on her leg.

He froze, then let out a breath, and relaxed. "Lacy, you have to stop looking at me like that every time I touch you."

"Like what?" she asked.

"Like I'm the villain in an old black and white movie who is going to tie you to the railroad tracks. I'm a touchy-feely person. This is how I am with everyone."

"You must be really popular on the force," she said.

He rolled his eyes. "This is how I am with women."

"I know; your reputation precedes you."

"Do you have a comeback for everything?" he asked.

"Yes."

"Of course you do," he said. Turning his attention back to the book, he leaned forward again. "Does anything else ring a bell?"

She too, leaned forward, but it was difficult to think clearly with his hand on her leg, his thumb making circles on the inside of her knee. The journal was divided into two columns. The right hand side appeared to be a list of items, and some of them she recognized from the house.

"Here." She tapped the book. "I saw these two perfumes in her bathroom. They're very expensive. And this might be the designer dress I saw in her closet." She looked up, staring thoughtfully into space. "I might be able to recognize more if I could take another look around her house."

"Don't even think about it," he said.

"I was just musing," she said defensively.

"Don't muse. My nerves can't take it." He gave her knee a gentle squeeze, and she jumped because it tickled. "Do any of the words in the left column make sense?"

Reluctantly, she ripped her attention from his face and turned back to the book. "Simon Says," she read out loud. "Feathers McGee." Those names were across from the two perfumes. "No, nothing about those words makes sense in any way. Those must be code for something else." Her watch alarm beeped, and she turned it off.

"What's that for?" he asked.

"Visiting hours at the jail." A glance at the clock showed it to be almost ten. Jason had arrived at eight. How had the time sped by so quickly?

"I guess that's my cue to leave," he said. "Thanks for breakfast, Lacy. It was good."

"Can I send you home with some prune cake?" she asked hopefully. She had to get it out of the house, the quicker the better.

"No thanks," he said. "Don't get me wrong; it was really good, and I liked it, but I try to watch what I eat."

"Me too," she said. *I watch it go in as quickly as possible, that is.*

"Walk me to the door," he commanded. Then he grasped her hand and led her behind him, not giving her the chance to refuse. Once there, he turned and slipped his arms around her, cinching her close. "We need to have a talk that's a little overdue."

Lacy's heart kicked into high gear. This was totally unexpected; Jason seemed like the kind of guy who would do anything possible to avoid talking about feelings, and yet here he was apparently initiating the conversation.

"What you were talking about earlier, the platonic thing, do you think we have a chance at being friends?" he asked, catching her by surprise.

He wanted to be friends with her? She had expected him to reiterate his earlier statement that they were all wrong for each other, to tell her she was a great girl, but she wasn't his type, to say he needed space. Asking to be friends was so shocking she at first had no reply. "I don't know," she said at last, drawing out the words.

"Because we can't seem to get along for more than five minutes at a time?" he asked.

"No. The fighting doesn't bother me. The touching does."

"This bothers you?" he gave her an emphatic squeeze.

She nodded. "This isn't how I relate to my friends. This seems more like dating."

"Don't you like it?" he asked.

"I like it too much," she replied honestly. "But it's not me. I'm not casual like this. I'm not touchy-feely."

"So maybe you'll come around to my way of thinking," he said.

Or maybe I'll fall in love with you. That thought, so horrible and scary, made her shiver. "I can't think clearly when we're like this," she said. As if to prove her point, her hands snaked up to clasp around his neck. "I don't like this foggy feeling when I'm around you. You make it hard to think straight."

"Pardon me if I take that as a compliment," he said cockily.

"But it's not," she argued. "I'm not the girl who has casual flings. I'm not the girl who plays with fire. I'm a thinker, a slow mover, a deliberate planner. I'm rational."

"Did it ever occur to you that I know these things about you already? And that, just maybe, that's what I want and need in my life right now? I'm tired of drama. I want a relationship that's not based purely on physical attraction. I want to try something new for once; I want to be friends."

The problem, she realized, was that as far as she was concerned their relationship *was* based purely on physical attraction, at least from her perspective. Even in the midst of this serious conversation, she was hyper aware of his hands on her, and her hands on him. "I don't know if I can do this," she said.

"Try. We can help each other. You can teach me how to be friends with a girl, and I can get you a little more comfortable with physical affection."

She groaned and dropped her head to his shoulder. "You don't get it at all," she said.

"I do," he insisted. "This is hard for me, too, refraining from kissing you right now. But I'm doing it. Maybe with time we'll get used to each other and it won't be so difficult."

But even as he said the words, all she could think was how his shoulder felt like warm granite. His hand smoothed up and down her spine, and the soothing touch, along with the powerful bunching of rock-hard sinew and muscle beneath her ear, made it difficult to think clearly.

"I'll try," she promised at last. "We'll be friends. But don't kiss me; kiss me and the deal is off."

"What if you kiss me?" he asked.

"The same goes if either of us kisses the other one."

"So, just to clarify, I not only have to make sure I don't kiss you, but I have to make sure you don't kiss me," he said.

"Those are the rules."

"I feel like we're twelve."

"So do I. When we were twelve, I had a huge crush on you."

He pulled back so he could see her face. "Does that mean you have a huge crush on me now?"

"I'm not answering that question." She gave his chest a light shove. "Go away."

He gave her an impish smile as he let himself out. "See you, pal."

"Later, buddy," she replied. She watched until his Jeep was out of sight, then she gathered up her keys and purse and went to visit her grandmother.

Chapter 11

The jail was crowded again, causing Lacy to wonder just how many people were incarcerated in their town. When it was her turn, she presented a large gourmet coffee to Travis who greeted her with a cheerful smile.

"You're a lifesaver," he said. "I slept four hours last night, and the coffee here is horrible."

She could have argued with him, telling him he was the lifesaver for getting her grandmother to agree to talk with her, but she didn't. There was a mercenary part of her that thought it might be better to leave him feeling in her debt. Maybe it was her journalistic instincts, but it was always good to have a cop source, and Jason had already made it clear he wouldn't be providing that service.

Lacy had never felt nervous in her grandmother's presence before, but she did now. Then again, she had never been rejected by her grandmother, never visited her in jail, never sat opposite her on one side of thick, bullet-proof glass.

If her grandma had shuffled in, looking old and defeated, Lacy would probably have broken down and run crying from the visitation room. But she didn't. Despite the ugly orange jumpsuit, her step was as spry and lively as ever, and she wore a smile on her face, even if it looked slightly strained and subdued.

"Hello, Lacy," she said, but Lacy could only read her lips. She pointed to the phone, and her grandmother looked at it in surprise before picking it up. "Just like on television," she said.

Lacy smiled. "I guess so. How are you doing, Grandma?"

"I'm fine, honey."

Lacy suppressed a sigh of impatience. How long could she keep up the charade? When would she realize Lacy was an adult, an equal, and not a child who had to be protected from the ugly realities of life?

"Why don't you tell me what happened?" Lacy suggested.

"There's nothing to tell," her grandmother insisted. "I didn't kill that woman."

"I know, Grandma, but I need to know why the police think you did. How long have you known Barbara Blake?"

"I don't know her, really. She was younger than me in school, and we ran in different circles then. She went to our church occasionally, and I always remember thinking she was such a pretty, vivacious girl."

"Why did you take her a pie?" Lacy asked.

"Well, it just seemed like the neighborly thing to do," her grandmother replied, which would have been a reasonable answer if her eyes hadn't shifted slightly to the right so as to avoid contact with Lacy.

"Grandma," Lacy pressed. "What happened on the day you went to visit her?"

"Nothing, Lacy," her grandmother said. "I took her the pie. We talked for a few minutes, and then I left."

"Did you stay to have pie with her?" Lacy asked.

"No, I didn't," her grandmother said and once again she was looking Lacy in the eye. "Everything happened exactly as I said. I took her the pie, followed her inside her house to set it on the counter. We talked briefly, and then I left."

"Did anyone see you leave? Did you go anywhere after her house?"

"I went straight home and began baking again." Her grandmother perked up. "It takes an hour to bake that cake. You got home at three that day. I remember because I had just taken it out of the oven. That means I put it in at two, and I would have had to start it sometime before that. Maybe you could check the woman's time of demise against what time the cake went in the oven."

Lacy smiled, stirring restlessly in her seat. Wouldn't it be ironic if her favorite cake provided her grandmother with an alibi? "I'll look into that, Grandma. Is there anything else you can tell me?

Did she tell you why she returned to town after such a long absence? What did you talk about with her that day?"

She watched as her grandmother's eyes slid to the side again. "This and that. I don't remember everything that was said."

"Grandma, please. You can't keep anything from me; this is too important. I'm not a baby anymore. I can help you."

"It's all going to be all right, dear. Truth will prevail; the Lord will work things out."

"Sometimes the Lord needs a little help," Lacy said.

Her grandmother's eyes snapped back to her face. "Lacy, don't talk like that. It's sacrilegious to presume the Lord needs us for anything. We're all at His mercy. If this is where He wants me to be right now, then this is where I'll stay."

Grandma had no tolerance for Lacy's more progressive and cynical views on religion, and Lacy had no interest in antagonizing her any further today. "I met the new pastor of your church."

The older woman perked up and leaned forward. "You did? What's he like?"

"Young and very sweet. We had dinner last night."

Lacy realized her mistake as soon as she said it. Her grandmother leaned forward a little more until she was in danger of smashing her face against the glass. "Oh really?" She was using the tone, the one that meant she smelled a potential mate for her granddaughter.

"It wasn't like that, Grandma."

"In my day it was always like that. It baffles me how young people today are able to be friends with each other. In my day you either got married, or you didn't. There was no middle ground."

"Weren't you friends with Grandpa before you married him?" Lacy asked.

"No. He asked me out when we were in high school, and that was that. We were married the day after graduation."

Lacy smiled at her grandmother's dreamy expression. Life seemed so much simpler then. Her grandmother had fallen in love,

94

gotten married, had a baby, and lived happily ever after until her husband died. And she was still so besotted with him that she had never chosen to remarry.

"Grandma, do you think you'll ever fall in love and remarry someday?"

Her grandmother laughed, causing a few other inmates to look at her in surprise. "No, sweetheart. Love is for the young; it's for people like you. Hint, hint."

Lacy couldn't help but smile. "Grandma, you're relentless."

"I just want to see you happy, Lacy." Her smile faltered.

"I'll be happy when you get out of here, and we can put this whole mess behind us."

"Well, to be honest, that will make me pretty happy too, dear. Now, listen, I don't want you getting involved in this mess. You can check with the policeman about the cake and the time of death, but that's it. I know you; don't go putting your foot in things. Promise?"

"No," Lacy said. "I'm sorry, Grandma, but I can't promise not to do everything possible to get you out of this."

"Lacy," her grandma began, but Lacy cut her off.

"If the situation were reversed, wouldn't you do everything possible to help me?"

"Of course I would, but it's not the same."

"It is the same," Lacy said. "You're my grandma and my best friend. You've been there for me the last few months while I was in horrible pain, and you haven't once told me I have to make up with Riley. Now it's my turn to be there for you unequivocally."

"Oh, Lacy." Her grandmother put her hand over her eyes and cried. "I don't want you involved in this."

"I'll be okay, Grandma."

"It's not only that I'm concerned for your safety. I'm afraid of what you might find out."

The last words were said so softly Lacy had to strain to hear them. "What? What are you talking about? What might I find out?"

"Nothing," her grandmother said. She wiped her eyes and sat up straight. "I should go now, dear. I'm tired. The good thing about this place is that they let us nap whenever we want." She tried and failed to find a smile. Instead, she pressed her palm to the glass. "I love you, Lacy. Nothing will ever change that."

"And nothing will ever change how much I love you, Grandma. Nothing."

Her grandmother put down the phone and stood, but not before Lacy caught her last two barely discernable words. "We'll see."

Lacy waved a halfhearted goodbye to Travis on her way out. The visit with her grandmother had been disconcerting to say the least. For the last few years, Lacy had wanted to be treated like a grownup and an equal where her grandparent was concerned, but now she was regretting that wish. Maybe she wanted to go back to the way it used to be--when her grandmother was almost superhuman in her perfection. Lacy couldn't think of one bad thing about the woman, and she didn't want to learn anything now that might mar the status quo.

But she realized she was being childish. Her grandma was human. Of course she had done bad, regrettable things in her life. Lacy should take the view that whatever she uncovered would only lend credence to the wise and wonderful woman she was now. Past mistakes didn't count if you had worked hard not to repeat them. If, on the off chance she discovered something negative, she vowed not to let it change things between them.

By the time she arrived home she was hungry and exhausted. Her early morning jog had made her hungrier than usual, despite the massive amounts of cake she'd consumed beforehand. And the emotional turmoil of the day had left her tired and drained. Instead of gorging herself on more cake, she ate a couple of tablespoons of peanut butter and an apple and lay down in her bed, Barbara Blake's journals at her side.

And once again she woke a couple of hours later with the journals still untouched beside her. The clock showed her it was time

96

to get ready for supper and the viewing with Tosh, so she stifled her frustration, rolled out of bed, and dressed in one of her ubiquitous black outfits. After living so long in New York, she could probably wear black every day for the next year and never repeat an outfit. Now that she was back in Middle America she needed to start incorporating some more color into her wardrobe or people would start to think she was depressed.

Of course, to buy clothes she needed money. And to get money she had to work. And in order to work, she needed time when she wasn't trying to solve the murder of a woman she had never met.

She was just finishing with her makeup when a knock sounded at the door. Grabbing her heels, she raced down the hall and skidded to a stop at the front door. "You're early," she said, flinging the door open with a smile.

"I am?" Jason asked. His uniform made him look larger so that he seemed to fill up the doorway. He scanned her up and down. "You look good in black." He rested his shoulder against the doorframe and leaned. "How serious are you about that no kissing policy?"

She knew he had only been on duty a little while. His hair was still damp from his shower, and it curled slightly around his ears. His cologne wafted through the open door, making her weak-kneed, and his almost indescribable multi-colored eyes sparked with intensity as he looked her over. Though his words had been teasing, Lacy found herself almost swaying toward him. *I wasn't serious at all; kiss me,* she wanted to say. Before she could conjure the words, though, a car door slammed. Jason turned to look as Tosh came loping up the sidewalk.

"You two have a date?" Jason muttered.

"We're going to the viewing."

Jason turned to look at her with a grimace. "Macabre choice."

She rolled her eyes. "He's the presiding pastor. He has to be there."

He leaned in to whisper hurriedly in her ear. "Don't tell him about the journals."

She frowned at him, not understanding the directive. "Too late."

"Lacy," he began, but it was all he had time for because suddenly Tosh was standing beside them, smiling.

"You look gorgeous," Tosh said.

"Thanks, but I wear this every day," Jason replied.

Tosh turned to him, unsmiling. "Officer Cantor."

Jason gave him a curt nod. "Pastor Underwood."

"And I'm Lacy Steele," Lacy added uncomfortably. "Now that we've reestablished our names, we should be going." Putting her hand on the doorframe for balance, she stepped into her heels, reached behind her for her purse, closed the door and stepped out.

Jason leaned around her and tried the door, sighing in frustration when he found it unlocked. "Lacy," he intoned.

"Sorry," she said. "I'll lock it." She reached for it, but he shooed her away.

"Just go. I'll check all the windows and doors. Have fun," he added sarcastically.

"We will," Tosh said sincerely. He clasped Lacy's hand and led her beside him, oblivious to the slamming of the front door. "For someone who's not dating you, he spends an awful lot of time near you."

"We're...friends," Lacy said, testing the new word as it applied to Jason.

Tosh opened the car door for her without further comment.

"What about you, Tosh," she said when he opened his door and slid behind the wheel. "Are you dating anyone?"

"You, apparently." He grinned at her.

Lacy laughed uncomfortably. He was kidding, wasn't he? Although this was their second night sharing dinner together, and this time felt even more like a date because they were both dressed up.

98

"Do you want to go back to the diner or somewhere else?" he asked.

"Somewhere else," she answered automatically. Two nights in a row at the diner was enough to make them regulars, and the topic of intense gossip.

"Is fast food okay?" He glanced at the clock. "I don't want to be late."

"Fast food is perfect." *And anonymous.* Lacy couldn't help but feel like the walls were closing in on her, especially after her chat with her grandmother this morning. As if reading her mind, Tosh asked her about it.

"How was your visit with your grandma?"

"Interesting. I told her about you, by the way."

He quirked an eyebrow and threw her a smile. "Did you now?"

"That you're the pastor of her new church," she added.

"Oh, that," he said, sounding disappointed.

"I should warn you that she's probably going to be picking out wedding patterns for us when she gets out of jail. Marrying a pastor would be her dream come true for me."

"But not for you?" he asked.

"I haven't given a lot of thought to marriage lately," she answered honestly. Not since her lying, cheating ex-fiancé dumped her for her sister.

"But your grandmother doesn't take your past into account?" he said sympathetically.

"No, but it's impossible to be upset with her when she's so sincere in her efforts. At least she stopped trying to fix me up with her friends' grandkids. That was awkward."

"I sense a good story. Tell me more."

"Well, there was the time she sent me on a blind date with Gladys Smith's grandson. He's forty, divorced, a proctologist, and wears a bad toupee."

"And you didn't marry him on the spot?" he said.

She shoved at his arm. "Don't laugh at me. It was horrible. And there was no easy way to explain to the meddling grandmothers why we didn't make an instant love connection."

"Any other misadventures in dating since you've been home?"

"Just one," she said, turning to stare outside the window.

"What was it?" his somber tone matched hers.

"The next guy she set me up with was much more my style-- young, handsome, a teacher."

"What happened?"

"Something he said reminded me of Robert. I burst into tears in the middle of supper and had to flee to the restroom. I couldn't stop crying. He took me home soon after."

"Uh-oh," Tosh said. "That's bad." He glanced at her again. "You didn't cry last night, and you're not crying now. Is that a sign that you've moved on?"

She shook her head. "It's a sign that you remind me nothing of Robert."

"And that's a good thing?" he asked.

"That's a very good thing," she agreed. "And the other positive outcome was that my grandmother realized I wasn't ready to date just yet. She backed off setting me up with people, although she still drops a whole lot of not-so-subtle hints."

"I want to visit her, but I've been tied up with funeral preparations. Do you think she'll see me in a couple of days?"

"She would never refuse a pastor anything," Lacy said. "She's wholly devoted to the church."

"I'm liking her more and more," Tosh said.

"You'll love her," Lacy said. "She's the best."

They arrived at the restaurant and once again Tosh waved off Lacy's offer to pay. "So tell me about Barbara Blake," he said when they received their food and sat down. "From what I can tell, there was no love lost for the woman in this community, and no one from New York has come forward, either."

"New York?" Lacy said, surprised. "That's where she's been living all this time?"

He nodded. "In some swanky apartment in Manhattan, although she didn't own it. Someone else had been paying the rent for her. I don't know who. Details are sketchy. That's why anything you can tell me will be helpful."

Lacy scanned her mind, trying to find *anything* that might be even slightly positive. "She had expensive taste. She seemed to enjoy the finer things in life. Her closet was like my every dream come true. Everything was a designer original. She must have been very wealthy."

Tosh shook his head. "From what I've been told, she didn't have a job."

Lacy frowned. "Then how did she get all the goods?"

Tosh laughed. "Do you always talk like you're in a gangster movie from the thirties?" He laughed again when she wrinkled her nose at him. "Maybe she had very kind admirers. Have you seen her? She's beautiful, even now. She doesn't look her age at all. If I didn't know how old she was, I would guess her to be in her fifties."

"Tosh, that's it," she said excitedly.

"What's it?"

"The journals. There was a list of possessions, and next to each item was a nonsensical name. I bet it's a list of what people gave her." She paused and tasted a fry. "But why would anyone keep a list like that?"

He shrugged. "Maybe she just liked lists. Lots of people do. Or maybe she had a reason for keeping track, like for thank-you notes."

"From what I know of her, she wasn't the type to send out thank-yous."

"Then maybe it was for blackmail."

"That's sinister, but a good possibility. Blackmail seems right down her alley. Maybe her admirers were married." She drummed her fingers on the table.

"There's really no way to know for sure without more information." Now it was his turn to stare thoughtfully at the fries. "Too bad we can't get back in the house. Sounds like another search is in order."

"You sound just like me, and, before you get your hopes up, that idea has already been nixed by Jason."

"Of course it has," Tosh said. "He's really living up to the reputation of a no- nonsense cop."

"And you're really killing the reputation of a blameless pastor."

"I was a guy long before I became a pastor, and I've always been the adventurous type. Strange that your boyfriend isn't."

"He isn't my boyfriend, and he was the adventurous type in school."

"So what happened to change him?"

"He really loves his career," Lacy answered, feeling somewhat defensive on Jason's behalf.

"So do I. Doesn't stop me from daydreaming about how the other half lives or what I would do if I weren't wearing a clerical collar."

Lacy chewed her chicken, thinking over Tosh's statement about Jason. From what she knew about him, she expected him to be a little bit wild. When had he become so careful and settled? Had something happened to alter his personality, or had her bad boy image always been incorrect? Was Jason more of a choirboy than she realized?

"Back to Barbara," Tosh said, recalling her attention. "She likes nice things and lists. Anything else? Did your grandmother say anything about her?"

"No. Grandma insists she didn't know her. She said she took her a pie to be neighborly."

"If she didn't know her, how did she know she was back in town?"

"You ask good questions, Tosh," Lacy said sincerely. Once again he was proving to be a good sounding board. "Let me write that one down so I can remember to ask Grandma, not like she'll tell me, though."

"You know, Lacy, there's a way to find out without asking," Tosh said. He continued speaking when she looked up at him. "You could search her things."

Lacy gasped. "You think I should spy on my grandma?"

"It sounds worse when you say it. I'm merely pointing out that you're doing your best to free her and she's standing in your way. It's possible that circumventing her might behoove you."

She blinked at him. "Did you just say 'behoove,' Pa Ingalls?"

He flicked her knuckle with his index finger. "Don't bite the hand that feeds you, Lacy." His finger lingered, smoothing gently over her knuckle, and she found the sensation not at all unpleasant. "So, back to Barbara."

"She had friends when she was here. She was on the homecoming court, so I guess that means she was probably popular in school. She held on to her parents' house all these years. That smacks of loyalty, I think."

"Or desperation," Tosh said. "She probably needed a backup plan in case her male admirers fell through."

"Tosh, you're supposed to be finding the silver lining within this information, remember?"

"You're right. But so far I don't think I like the picture I'm getting of this woman. She sounds like a conniving user."

"That's pretty much what her group of high school friends said about her. Maybe I can talk to them again tonight and try to wheedle a few positive attributes."

"I would appreciate that," Tosh said. "Otherwise I'm going to have to revert to my emergency backup sermon."

"What's your emergency backup sermon?" she asked.

"Reading a children's book. Don't laugh; it works every time to make people cry. You choose a touching book about a puppy who dies, or something, and anyone who actually cared about Barbara can apply it to her. Then you read a few verses from Ecclesiastes and--bam!--you're done."

Lacy laughed and shook her head. "Tosh, you're not like any pastor I've ever met before."

"And that's a good thing?" he guessed.

"That's a very good thing," she assured him. She and God hadn't exactly been on speaking terms lately, but if someone like Tosh believed the things her grandmother had been teaching her all her life, then maybe there was some truth to them.

"That reminds me. Do you attend my new church?" Tosh asked. He rested his head in his hand in what was becoming a familiar gesture to her while his eyes probed her face, searching for she knew not what.

"I haven't gone much since I've been back."

"Maybe now is a good time to start," he said.

"Maybe so," she agreed. They shared a smile then he checked his watch and hopped out of the booth.

"We have to book it," he said. "Ready?"

"Ready," she said. Somehow by the time they reached the car, they were holding hands, and Lacy had no idea how it happened. Why was touching Tosh second nature while touching Jason felt like an electric jolt every time? With him she was sure she would never look down and be surprised to realize she was holding on to him; she would know the second his hand touched hers. What was it that made her reaction to the two men so different and, more important, which way did she prefer?

Chapter 12

They were the first ones at the funeral home.

"Do you want to see her?" Tosh asked.

"I suppose," Lacy said. Her discomfort over viewing a dead body was overpowered by her curiosity about Barbara Blake. Who was this woman who had no mourners?

Once again Tosh took her hand, but this time he tucked it securely between both his in a comforting gesture that both reassured her and made her feel like a little girl. Slowly they walked together up to the casket. Lacy felt an odd pang at her first sight of the dead woman, but since it was the same initial feeling she always had when approaching a deceased person she chalked it up to anxiety.

Tosh hadn't been exaggerating; Barbara Blake was beautiful. Her skin was taught and flawless. Her blond hair was perfectly streaked with highlights and lowlights, making the color appear natural. If not for telltale age spots and wrinkles on her hand, Lacy would have guessed her age to be fiftyish. She studied the woman, trying in vain to find some clue about her from her appearance. Why had someone killed her? How had she gone through life with no connections?

She had no idea how long they stood there, staring, but eventually voices sounded from behind them. People began streaming in, some of them Lacy recognized. They came forward and only then did Lacy realize they thought she and Tosh were the receiving line.

"I'm so sorry for your loss," an elderly gentleman said, shaking her hand.

Lacy blinked at him in surprise. How did she get herself out of this awkward situation?

"That's so kind," Tosh answered. "But we aren't family. I'm the pastor of the church where she was a member." He didn't explain Lacy's presence, but the man drew his own conclusion.

"Oh, I heard we had a new pastor in town. You look too young to be a pastor, but I guess if you're old enough to be married, you're old enough to pastor a church."

Lacy's discomfort increased another notch, but Tosh draped his arm over her shoulder and smiled. "Pleased to meet you," he said. After the man moved on, he leaned down to whisper in Lacy's ear. "We've got to get away from here and circulate before people start asking us when we're planning to have children."

She smiled, patted his chest, and they moved apart, deciding they could learn more by separating than if they stayed together and drew questions of their own. Lacy wasn't surprised to see her grandmother's group of friends arrive. Not only was attending the viewing the proper thing to do, but the women would no doubt want to see what their former friend looked like now. *Unless one of them had already seen her,* Lacy thought. Remembering how nervous and shocked they had all been that first morning after the arrest, Lacy wondered again what their story was. What were they hiding? Was it possible that one of them had killed Barbara?

Lacy edged closer, picked up a bulletin, and pretended to study it while secretly eavesdropping on the group.

"She looks good," Gladys said grudgingly.

"She always did," Rose said. She pulled a handkerchief from her ample bosom and dabbed at the sweat on her upper lip. Everything about Rose was ample, from her pudgy body to her booming voice.

"Looks were never her problem," Maya said. "It was always her personality."

"Not that any man could understand that," Janice added peevishly.

"Yes, but she remained alone, and we were all happily married," Gladys pointed out.

Rose harrumphed. "You really think she was alone? You know what she was like."

Gladys looked around. "Shh, not so loud. It's disrespectful to speak ill of the dead, especially at their own viewing."

"There's nothing positive to say about this one, and you know it," Rose argued.

"At least she was funny sometimes," Janice said.

"At our expense," Maya added. "She had the meanest, most cutting sense of humor of anyone I've ever met, and she was so conniving that you never knew she was making fun of you until after the fact."

"Do you think anyone ever really knew her?" Gladys asked, staring hard at Barbara.

"If they did, she would either have been locked up in prison or a mental institute," Rose snapped.

Gladys blanched. "Rose, don't ever say that again."

Rose glanced around, too, caught Lacy's stare, and flushed. "Let's move along, ladies. We've done our duty and paid proper respect."

Curious, Lacy thought, *but not much new information to glean from.* Across the room, she spotted Tosh circulating around and talking to everyone in his path. How apropos that she was hiding out in a corner while he was being social. Where would Jason fit in if he were here, she wondered, but didn't have to think about it too long. He would be standing in the entryway, surveying the room and reading people's faces. Only after he decided the room was safe and the people trustworthy would he enter and begin to make polite conversation.

Lacy edged farther into the shadows until she was half hidden behind a large palm plant. Her hiding place gave her an unobscured view of the room, but if anyone turned and saw her inhaling palm fronds she would be mortified. Just as she was debating staying put or moving back toward the center of the room, a solitary figure slunk toward the open casket. Lacy froze, blinking in surprise as her old high school principal, Mr. Middleton, stopped short in front of Barbara Blake.

His lips moved as if he was talking, but Lacy was too far to hear what he was saying. And even if she was close enough to hear, she wouldn't have listened. Some things were too private--graveside conversations included.

How did Mr. Middleton know Barbara Blake? Had they been in the same class together? How old was he, anyway? He had always seemed ancient to Lacy, and she wasn't sure her opinion was off base. Not only had he been her high school principal, but he had been the principal when her mother was in high school, too. In fact, the rumor was that he would still be working if the school system hadn't forced him to retire the year after Lacy's sister, Riley, graduated.

What was the inscrutable expression on his face? A stoic man, his face didn't usually give much away, but now there was a glimmer of...what? Sadness? Had he loved Barbara? Was he the only true mourner in this room? If so, how sad. She could have stayed here, married this stable man, and possibly had a chance to change her selfish ways. Instead she had moved to New York and seemingly kept a detailed list of gifts from her male suitors.

Mr. Middleton turned from the casket and caught sight of Lacy. She froze like a deer in headlights when they made eye contact. His mouth opened slightly in what looked like surprise. He took a step toward her before thinking better of the idea. Instead he took a few steps back before turning to flee the room as if hounds were chasing him.

After that, things were uneventful. The mourners cleared out quickly, much sooner than the allotted visiting hours. Tosh finished talking to every person in the room, including the undertaker, and then came to fetch Lacy.

Placing his hand on the small of her back, he guided her from the house and toward his car. "How did it go? Did you learn anything new?"

"Mr. Middleton was here," she told him.

"Who's that?"

108

"My high school principal. He isn't the type to go to visiting hours willy-nilly. He must have known her somehow."

"So ask him how."

"I can't do that," she said.

"Why not?"

She shrugged. "He's so…intimidating. He scares me a little."

"What do you think he's going to do to you? Give you a suspension? It's a little late for that," he said, opening her car and holding her hand to help her inside.

"You don't understand. He's always had this way of looking at me like he knows what I'm thinking. It's creepy."

"My principal was like that, too," Tosh said. "But high school was a long time ago. Maybe he's lonely and would enjoy the opportunity to talk to a former student."

She shook her head. "You don't know Mr. Middleton."

"Neither do you," he pointed out. "Start small. Say hello next time you see him."

"I can probably manage a hello."

"Thatta girl," Tosh said cheerfully.

"Tosh, does anything ever depress you?" she asked.

"Yes," he said, not elaborating further. "And, see, I can be mysterious, too." He wagged his eyebrows at her, and she smiled.

They reached her house a few minutes later. It looked dark, lonely, and empty without her grandmother. "Want to come in and pick up the cake I promised you?" she asked, suddenly desperate not to be alone.

"Sounds good," he said. He followed her inside and stood looking around in the entryway. "Don't take this the wrong way, but it looks like an old lady lives here."

"I'm going to tell my grandmother you said that," she told him.

"From what you've told me I can do no wrong because I'm a pastor. I have carte blanche."

"True, but I wouldn't test the theory. At the very worst she won't bake for you, and that's a dire punishment."

"Fine, then, the house is very homey."

She paused and looked around, too. "It is, isn't it? It's always been my second home."

"Do your parents still live in town?"

"No, they've lived in Florida the past couple of years since they retired."

"Do you have aunts, uncles or cousins nearby?"

She shook her head. "My mom is an only child. I have some extended cousins that my grandma took under her wing, but that's about it. What about you?"

"I've never been under your grandmother's wing," he said.

She cut a piece of cake for him, using every drop of willpower to deny one for herself. He followed her to the couch, and they sat side by side while he ate.

"I'm from a large family. They're very devoutly Catholic. I didn't feel the liturgical vibe and wanted to go protestant. It's always good for the family outcast to gain physical distance from the rest of the family, don't you think?" he asked.

"Our family is too small for outcasts," she reminded him. "I think that's more of a big family type thing."

"How long has it been since you talked to your sister?" he asked.

"Over a year. Don't tell me I need to forgive her, Tosh."

"Wouldn't dream of it," he said. "Let's watch a movie. Does your grandmother have anything that doesn't have Charlie Chaplin in it?"

"She doesn't have any movies, but I do. I have to get them from my room, though. What are you in the mood for?"

"Surprise me," he said.

"French subtitles it is," she said, starting to rise.

He caught her hand and pulled her back. "Don't surprise me. Find a comedy."

110

"All right," she agreed. She returned a few minutes later with said comedy, and put it in the DVD player. The rest of the world had upgraded to newer and better technology, but her grandmother had only gotten a DVD player a year ago.

She sat on the couch, close to Tosh, and he put his arm around her. Her natural instinct was to move closer and rest her head on his shoulder, and so she did, not bothering to wonder again why she felt so comfortable with him. She just did. She felt as if she had known him forever instead of for two days.

Some time later, he whispered in her ear. "Lacy, wake up."

Her eyes opened slowly, blinking in confusion. "I fell asleep?"

"Almost after the opening credits," he said.

"You could have woken me sooner," she mumbled, stifling a yawn.

"I didn't mind," he said. His arm was still around her, but she had slipped farther into his embrace until he was almost cradling her. They studied each other a few beats before he spoke again. "It's late. I should go. I'll see you tomorrow at the funeral."

"Okay," she agreed.

"I'll see myself out." He eased away from her and stood, backing toward the door in almost the same way that Mr. Middleton had walked away from the casket earlier. He didn't turn until he stepped onto the porch, and then he faded into the darkness. She heard the hum of his car engine and she stood, securing the door and turning off the light.

When she turned to walk down the hallway toward her room, she found that she didn't feel sleepy anymore. Instead, she was wide awake. Thoughts of the waiting journals drew her toward her room, but then something Tosh had said gave her pause outside her grandmother's room.

You could search her things.

Lacy stood outside her grandmother's room, biting her lip in indecision, hating what she was contemplating. Like her, her grandma valued privacy. Lacy had never before dreamed of invading that

111

sacred trust, and she had no doubts that her grandmother had ever entertained thoughts of snooping through Lacy's belongings. But Tosh was right. She needed to help her grandmother any way she could. Unlocking the key to her connection with the dead woman might be the solution to getting her out of jail.

Guiltily, slowly, she crept into the room. It smelled just like her grandma, like peppermint and vanilla. Lacy stopped short in the doorway, her reticence kicking into high gear once again. *I'm doing it for her own good,* she repeated over and over to herself, and that thought inched her forward until she reached her grandmother's nightstand.

Somehow Lacy knew that everything her grandmother held dear and personal was kept in that square piece of furniture. With shaking fingers, she reached out and pulled open the bottom drawer. In it she found cards and letters from her, her sister, and her mother, as well as from her deceased grandfather. Everything in this drawer was beginning to yellow with age, telling Lacy that it hadn't been used lately.

Without rifling through, she closed the bottom drawer and opened the top one. At first, she thought she must be mistaken about the timeline of the drawers because there was an envelope marked, "Our first five years." Inside were several old receipts, ticket stubs, menus, a few canceled checks--one of them quite large--and a couple of letters. Lacy scanned the letters, but quickly realized they were all from her grandfather. She was vaguely curious about the contents of the envelope. Obviously they chronicled her grandparents' first five years of married life, and even from a non-personal standpoint Lacy found the information fascinating. It was like history come to life.

But she forced herself to put the envelope away. Either her grandmother would share it with her when she wanted, or Lacy would go through it after her death. In any case, it wasn't relevant to the situation at hand.

Just when she was about to give up hope, she found a handwritten note stuffed in the front of the drawer. The paper and

112

ink looked new, and the double B's in the signature jumped out at Lacy.

"Lucinda, I'm back in town and eager to talk to you about our little pet project. See me at your earliest convenience, or else. Barbara Blake."

What pet project? What did the menacing "or else" mean? There was no way Lacy's grandmother was involved in anything illegal, but the letter certainly held a sinister undertone. And it had obviously worked to compel Lucinda Craig to visit, probably almost as soon as she received the threatening letter.

Then another horror dawned on Lacy. She was holding evidence against her grandmother in her hand. Barbara had made a threat, if not explicit, then certainly implied. Whatever this letter was about could be enough motive for a conviction. If the obnoxious Detective Brenner ever got a warrant to search this house, then her grandmother would be up a creek.

Without further thought about what she was doing, Lacy took the note to the bathroom, lit it on fire, dropped it in the sink, and washed away the ashes, allowing the water to run for a long time, just to make sure everything went all the way down. Then she returned to her grandmother's room and began searching in earnest, looking for she knew not what. But if she found anything remotely incriminating, she would get rid of that, too. Her grandmother didn't murder that woman, and she wouldn't allow anything to be misconstrued as proof that she had.

An hour later, after desperately searching every nook and cranny and then putting everything back together, Lacy fell into bed exhausted. Not even bothering to wash her face, she fell into a deep and dreamless sleep.

Chapter 13

For the third day in a row, Lacy woke just after the sun rose. Frustrated that her exhaustion hadn't resulted in more sleep, she picked up her pillow and ground it into her face.

But when she remembered all she had to do, she rolled out of bed. After yawning so often in the shower she was in danger of drowning, she realized she was in need of mass quantities of coffee. Since her schedule was so busy, she dressed for the funeral, loaded her bag with her computer and the journals, and drove to the coffee shop. Driving to the small café a few blocks away wasn't part of her routine, so after she walked halfway there, Lacy had to go back and get the car.

As usual, the shop was crowded and the bran was sold out. Lacy irritably wondered why they didn't scrap all the other flavors of muffins and put all their efforts into producing more bran, by far the fan favorite. Of course that meant there would be no chocolate chip muffins for her, and that would be sad.

Before she could muster the words to order, Peggy presented her with a chocolate chip muffin and large coffee--her standard order.

"Peggy, I love you," Lacy mumbled as she handed Peggy her money.

Peggy laughed and tucked the money into the cash register. "Hope the day gets better from here, Lacy."

"Thanks," Lacy said, though she had no idea if Peggy heard her because another, older person had already taken her place in line.

She was almost finished with her coffee before she finally started to perk up. She pulled out one of the journals and picked up where she had left off, reading the list of items and mentally keeping a tally of how much they were worth. When her mental tally reached a million dollars, she put the book facedown on the table, feeling sick to her stomach.

114

The coffee shop hit a lull. Peggy appeared before Lacy, offering a refill.

"Thanks," Lacy said. If Peggy noticed her dismal tone, she didn't comment on it before skittering back to the counter when a new group of customers arrived.

Lacy began to look around the coffee house, wondering if anyone else was dressed in funeral wear. As she was making her inspection, Rose, Janice, Maya, and Gladys trooped in as a unit. They were all jabbering, and all dressed in black. Once again Rose was the first to notice Lacy. She nudged the two ladies standing nearest to her, and they turned toward Lacy jointly as if there were hidden ropes that tethered them together.

Lacy smiled and waved. As soon as they received their food, they plodded over to her and stopped in front of her table.

"I've never seen you guys in here before," she said.

"Today is going to be a long day," Rose said. "We thought it would be nice to relax before the big event."

Lacy tried not to wince at the way Rose made the funeral sound like a demolition derby.

"Why are you going?" Rose asked, nodding toward Lacy's black dress.

"She knew my grandmother," Lacy said, trying to rattle them with that information. Did they know about the connection between the two women? Were they covering for her grandmother?

"She did?" Rose asked in genuine surprise. "Lucinda wasn't one of our original set in high school. Even if she had been our age, she was always too mature and sensible for the likes of us. We were boy crazy and immature. Lucinda always had marriage and family on her mind."

If Lacy hadn't been staring directly at them, she wouldn't have noticed Maya and Janice elbow Rose in an attempt to shut her up.

Rose is chatty, Lacy noted, filing the information away for a later purpose. She had a feeling she wasn't done wringing

115

information from this bunch. From what she could tell, they were the people in town who knew Barbara best. Who's to say one of them wasn't still in contact with her? Why else would she have returned from New York after so long an absence if it wasn't to reconnect with someone in the community?

"A table opened up," Janice said. "Let's go, Rose." She clamped her hand on Rose's elbow and practically dragged her to the waiting table.

Lacy picked up the journal again, but almost immediately a new shadow fell over her. "Mr. Middleton," she said with a yelp of surprise. He stood to her right, frowning down at her.

"Why is a young girl like you wasting your time hanging around at viewings and funerals?"

Lacy was so surprised by the question that she blinked at him a few times. Why did it sound like he earnestly cared about her wellbeing? She had always thought of him as a stern disciplinarian, a loner who had no time for marriage or a family of his own. But maybe Tosh was right; maybe she had misjudged him. Did he think of his many former students as his children? Was he secretly lonely and longing for some companionship?

"Would you like to sit down?" she found herself asking.

Now it was his turn to blink at her in surprise. "Okay." He pulled out the chair across from her, scraping it loudly on the ground. He sat and they stared at each other.

"I didn't know you knew Barbara Blake," she blurted, trying desperately to fill the awkward silence.

"I know everyone in this town," he said. His voice was more gravelly than she remembered. For an older man, he had retained his good looks. He was what her grandmother would call distinguished looking with his white hair and spiffy clothing.

"Were you a principal when she was in school?"

He shook his head. "We grew up together. I was four years older than her. Our parents were friends."

There was another awkward pause while they studied each other and then he spoke again.

"I was sorry to hear about your grandmother. The police in this town are a bunch of fools if they believe Lucy could murder anyone."

Two conflicting thoughts warred in her head, tumbling to get out. "Not all the cops are bad, and you know my grandmother?"

One lip curled in the semblance of a smile. "I told you I know everyone. Your grandmother is a nice lady. And you're correct: Jason Cantor is a good officer." He sipped his coffee and gave her a knowing glance.

Her cheeks warmed with a blush. Somehow it was more embarrassing to talk to this man about Jason than it was with anyone else. Probably because she had thought of him as a loveless soul who knew nothing about romance. But apparently she had been wrong.

"I'm sorry your friend died. I think you might be the only person in town who is mourning her."

"I'm not mourning her," he bit off. "She was a horrible person, and I'm glad she's dead."

Lacy gasped. Mr. Middleton cleared his throat. "I shouldn't have said that. I'm not glad she's dead, but she was a horrible person, and I don't mourn her. But proper respect needs to be paid. Goodness knows no one is going to cry for an old codger like me when I'm gone, but I hope people will do the right thing by me and show up anyway."

It was the most Lacy had ever heard him say at any one time. Previously her experience with him had been limited to hearing him yell a misbehaving kid's name down the hallway at school. And it had always had the effect of causing the kid to freeze in his tracks, a look of sheer terror on his face.

"How's your sister?" he asked, taking another sip of his coffee.

"She's fine." Now it was Lacy's turn to adopt a clipped tone.

Mr. Middleton took another sip of his coffee. "Sisters shouldn't fight."

She tipped her head, perplexed. "How did you know Riley and I aren't speaking?"

"Old principals with nothing else to do know everything, Lacy," he said. Then he did the unthinkable: he winked and smiled at her, a real, warm smile that looked as cheerful as Santa Claus on Christmas morning. He lumbered slowly to his feet. "See you at the funeral."

Lacy had no reply. Mouth agape with surprise, she watched him slowly walk out the door and down the street.

A few minutes later, after she had fully recovered her senses, she looked at the clock on the wall and realized it was almost time for her meeting with Detective Brenner. She hopped in her grandmother's Buick and drove to the jail.

The detective had been unavailable to meet with her yesterday after her visit. Instead she had set an appointment for first thing this morning. She arrived a few minutes early, and his secretary told her he wasn't in yet. Impatiently, she sat on her hands, twisting back and forth and waiting for her name to be called.

Raucous male laughter sounded from down the hall. She craned her neck around the doorway and saw the detective, sipping his coffee and talking to another employee.

"I see him," Lacy said to the secretary. "Can you tell him I'm here, please?"

"I told him ten minutes ago," the secretary said. She sounded longsuffering, and Lacy felt no small amount of pity for her. What must it be like to work for someone so rude and overbearing?

Lacy loudly cleared her throat in the vain attempt that the detective would look her way. At last when it was either speak to him now or be late for the funeral, she stood and marched through the door, coming face to face with the detective. Whomever he had been talking to scurried into a nearby office, closing the door firmly behind him.

118

"Detective, we had an appointment twenty minutes ago," Lacy said.

He stared at her or, rather, he stared down at her--most likely trying to intimidate her with his superior height and girth. But Lacy wasn't intimidated; she was angry. This man was responsible for inflicting emotional harm on her sweet and delicate grandmother. If necessary, she would take him on in a physical fight to the death if that was what was needed to make him listen to her. When he realized she wasn't quavering in fear before him, he relaxed his position slightly.

"What do you want to talk to me about?"

"It's about my grandmother. I want to know Ms. Blake's time of death."

"I can't release that information."

"That information is public property. I could get a lawyer to draft a notice on the Freedom of Information Act, or you could simply tell me what I already have the right to know."

He stood staring at her a moment longer, probably deciding how far he wanted to take his resistance. Was everything a battle with this man?

"The coroner puts the time of death sometime between noon and three."

"My grandmother put a cake in the oven at two. It's a laborious, time consuming recipe that takes a half hour to put together, at the very least, making the time she arrived home one thirty at the latest. According to your witness, the neighbor I talked to myself, my grandmother arrived at the dead woman's house at eleven AM. Wouldn't it make sense that she would kill her immediately and flee as quickly as possible? Yet according to your expert the murder time wasn't until at least an hour after my grandmother arrived. And then there's the matter of the cake she baked for me."

"So you say," he said. "How am I to believe there even was a cake?"

"It was sitting on the table when you arrived to arrest her. Didn't you smell sugar and cinnamon the minute you walked in?"

He rolled his eyes. "Go home, Miss Steele. Leave the police work to the professionals."

"I would if I could find one," she retorted. "There are so many holes in your case it looks like Swiss cheese, and yet you refuse to see differently. My grandmother didn't do it. She had no motive. She has an alibi."

"A cake is not an alibi," he said. "And we have witnesses."

"Witnesses who saw her arrive an hour before the murder took place," Lacy said. "And she admitted to being there, but she was only there to drop off that pie."

"And the murder weapon had that very pie on it," the detective said smugly.

"But did it have my grandmother's fingerprints or DNA? Were either of those things found on the plates or glasses? No, because she didn't stay to eat the pie. She dropped it off and left it, just like she said." Saying the words out loud made her think of another question. "Whose prints and DNA were on the plates? Who did she have pie with?"

The detective shifted uncomfortably. "The DNA on the plates came back to a man. No discernable prints or DNA were found on the knife, except that of the victim."

Lacy blinked at him. "You mean to tell me that you have male DNA, and yet you're holding my grandmother because she's the one who baked a pie."

"Obviously there was some sort of love triangle going on. Your grandmother killed Miss Blake in a fit of jealous rage."

And that was the moment Lacy snapped. "Are you insane?" she yelled. "What is wrong with you? That's the stupidest piece of garbage I've ever heard. My grandmother has dated and loved exactly one man in her entire life, and he's buried in a cemetery that has her name on the tombstone beside his. You will not be able to find one witness who will testify that my grandmother was interested in a man.

120

In some ways I almost hope this case goes to trial because then the world will be able to see what a fool of a buffoon you really are."

His face was puce by the end of her speech. He took a step toward her and leaned over, shoving his index finger in her face. "You listen to me, little girl. I'm going to give you the chance to walk out of here right now. If you're not gone in the next thirty seconds, I'm going to arrest you for obstruction of justice and threatening a police officer. The clock is ticking."

She opened her mouth to unleash on him again when a hand clamped firmly over her lips. Another arm came around her waist and forcibly lifted her from the ground, dragging her backwards out of the room.

When Jason set her down outside the building, she rounded on him.

"What are you doing? How can you possibly take his side?"

"I'm not taking his side, Lacy. I'm keeping you out of jail. He wasn't kidding about arresting you. He levels those charges at anyone who disagrees with him, and he would have had me cuff you just because he's that mean and petty." He ran his hands through his hair, causing it to stand on end. "What are you thinking? Can't I leave you alone for a minute without you getting yourself into hot water? You can't go around yelling at the second most powerful man in the county that way. He's not the sort of man you want as an enemy."

"What am *I* thinking? What are *you* thinking? How can you swallow your pride and wallow in the misery he emits, day after day?"

"Because I don't have the luxury of letting him have it and then walking away. I work here. I work for him." For emphasis, he pointed his finger toward the building. "Like it or not, he's my boss. What happened to miss 'I'm not emotional, I'm a planner, I'm a thinker, I'm rational?'"

Hearing him toss her words back in her face had an oddly cooling effect on her. It was no secret that she had a raging bad temper, but she had always respected law and authority before. She looked Jason up and down while she thought. He was dressed in civilian clothes and his hair was in wild disarray. Not to mention that his hands were fisted on his hips, his feet spread wide in a fighting stance, and he was scowling at her. She couldn't help it; she giggled.

His scowl deepened. "What are you laughing at?"

"You. Me. Us. This whole absurd situation. I mean, two weeks ago I could never have imagined myself yelling at a detective because he arrested my grandmother for murder." Another giggle bubbled up and she suppressed it. "What are you doing here, anyway?" He didn't begin work until noon, and it was only a little after nine.

"I heard through the rumor mill that you had this appointment today. Color me clairvoyant, but I thought something like this might happen."

"Did you just roll out of bed?" she asked, ignoring his backhanded insult.

"I work second shift," he reminded her. "Most nights I'm not in bed until after two." He swiped a weary hand down his face before resting his arm on her shoulders and turning her toward the parking lot. "C'mon. Do you have time to grab a cup of coffee?"

"I'd better not. I've already had four cups today. And I have a funeral to attend."

They reached her car and faced each other. "Do you really think you're going to learn something by going to her funeral?" he asked.

"No, but it's not about that anymore. This woman died all alone in the world, and no one cares. I feel like I need to go because someone needs to be witness to her passing. Does that make sense?"

"It does, and it also proves you are as sweet and lovely as I thought you might be."

She smiled up at him, enjoying the sight of his sleep-swollen eyes and tousled hair. "Why don't you go home and get some more sleep? You look tired."

"I am tired," he said, sounding groggy.

Before she could talk herself out of it, she put her hands on his chest, leaned in, and kissed his cheek. "Thanks for coming to get me." When she pulled away he was staring at her, dumbfounded.

"I thought you said no kissing," he said.

"Cheeks don't count." She winked at him, and gave him a little wave before turning to duck into her car. He caught her wrist, holding her in place.

"Lacy, what's gotten into you this morning?"

I don't want to die alone like Barbara Blake and Mr. Middleton. "Maybe it's all the coffee I drank." Her flippant tone was sharp contrast to her inner turmoil. Already it had been an emotionally draining morning, and she still had a funeral to attend.

"Then by all means let's get you one of those hats with two cups and a straw. We'll keep you caffeinated all day long."

She laughed, feeling some of the weight shift slightly away from her chest. She started her car and poked her head out the window. "Did I get you in trouble with him?" She bit her lip and looked worriedly toward the building.

Jason leaned down and pressed his palm to her cheek. "Don't worry about it; I'll be fine. You take care."

For a split second she closed her eyes and leaned in to his touch. Then she opened her eyes, blinked back a few tears, and sped away, leaving Jason standing in the parking lot with his hand still outstretched.

Chapter 14

The funeral was a small gathering. Lacy sat by herself off to the side and watched as her grandmother's friends wandered in, along with Mr. Middleton, and a handful of people she didn't know.

Tosh took the platform, looking very clerical in his black robe and white collar. His eyes sifted the crowd until they rested on Lacy, and they shared a brief smile before the service began.

He gave the facts of Barbara Blake's life and paused as if uncertain how to continue. Then he pulled out a children's book and commenced reading. Lacy remembered how, yesterday, she had laughed when he proposed the idea of reading a children's book, but she found no humor in the actuality. Instead, a great sadness came to settle somewhere over her heart, pressing down on her like a boulder. How tragic that the end of this woman's life was summed up by a book about a lost puppy, and how horrible that no one seemed to care.

All over the church people sat dry-eyed, looking almost bored, all except Mr. Middleton who once again had that unreadable expression on his face. He was the only person in the room showing any emotion, except for Lacy who found to her shock that she was crying.

Well, good. Someone needed to cry for this woman. Even if she had been a horrible person, she had once been someone's little girl. Everyone, good or bad, deserved to have at least one genuine mourner at their funeral.

Unfortunately, Lacy's supply of tears ran dry before they did anything to ease the odd ache in her chest. She had a feeling that the press of anxiety wouldn't go away until her grandmother was out of jail, and maybe not even then. Somewhere in the back of her mind, she knew part of her problem was the fact that she needed to make up with her sister, but she wasn't ready for that yet--not by a long shot. Until she was, there would always be a part of her that felt unsettled and restless, as if there was something she was missing.

The service ended and the church emptied. Lacy didn't want to file past the body, but she did because it was procedure, and she lacked the emotional stamina to buck tradition. Once outside the building, she leaned against the bricks, drawing deep breaths and trying to cleanse her nose from the stench of lilies. When she opened her eyes and looked around, the parking lot was nearly deserted. Had the procession left without her?

But, no, there was no procession. Tosh joined her a moment later and lightly touched her elbow.

"Where did everyone go?" she asked.

"They left," he said. "There are only a few people going to the gravesite. Lacy, you don't have to do this."

"Yes I do," she said.

"Then at least ride with me." He kept his hand on her elbow and used it to guide her to the car, opening the passenger door for her when they reached it.

Once settled inside the car, he reached for her hand and clasped it, resting their combined hands on her knee.

"Performing a funeral is much harder than I thought it would be," he said. His tone was somber, and Lacy was thankful. She wouldn't have been able to stand it if he had been his usual jovial, carefree self.

"You're doing a great job," she said. She gave his hand a comforting squeeze.

He turned to smile at her. "It helps having you here. I don't know why you're doing this, but I'm glad."

"Someone needs to be sad this woman is gone," she said.

"It seems like your principal is. Besides you, he's been the most stalwart attendee. He's coming to the graveside, too."

"He's not sad," Lacy blurted.

"Then what is he?"

"I don't know," she said. *Relieved,* was the first word that popped into her mind, but she didn't know why. If Mr. Middleton and Barbara Blake had grown up together, why would he possibly be relieved at her passing?

They arrived at the cemetery, and Mr. Middleton was the only other person in attendance. He and Lacy stood beside each other while Tosh read the requisite scripture, and then it was over.

"Wait," Lacy said, causing the two men to look at her in surprise. She searched her mind for something, anything personal she could say about this woman. "Barbara Blake was beautiful. She took excellent care of herself, and she liked nice things. She had excellent taste in clothes, shoes, and perfume. She was very memorable. Even after a fifty year absence, people in this town never forgot her. And she held on to her parents' house, which says something good about her, I think," Lacy said. She was grasping at straws and she knew it.

Beside her, Mr. Middleton stared at her like she was crazy, and then he faced forward and began to talk, too. "Barbara was always beautiful, since the day she was born. She could light up the room with her smile. Her laugh was like a bell and she turned heads wherever she went. She always had impeccable style, and there was one thing she did right in her life, one thing that I'll always be grateful for."

Tosh looked between them to make sure they were done, and then he picked up a handful of dirt and tossed it on the grave. "'Earth to earth, ashes to ashes, dust to dust; in sure and certain hope of the Resurrection into eternal life.'" And then it was over. Mr. Middleton walked away without a backward glance, and Lacy and Tosh walked to his car.

"I'll take you home," Tosh said. "You can get your car from the church later."

"All right." The church was only a few blocks away. She could walk there and pick it up at any time. But not now; right now she was weary. She just wanted to go home, change into something comfortable, and possibly send herself into a sugar coma with prune cake.

But that wasn't to be. Lacy was in such a daze, she didn't notice that the front door was ajar, but Tosh did. He put his arm around her and swept her behind him. Using his elbow, he pushed the door all the way open and called out.

"Hello, anyone in there? We're home; now's the time to run away."

When there was no answer, he took a tentative step inside, Lacy so close on his heels that she held onto the back of his shirt to avoid bumping into him. They inched into the house as Tosh called out a few more warnings, but there was no answering sound from inside.

"Whoever was here is long gone, and they left a mess behind," Tosh said. "I'm sorry, Lacy."

She stepped around him to get the full effect and gasped. The house had been tossed. When she was little and refused to clean her room, her mother used to say that it looked like a cyclone had hit it. Now Lacy understood what that meant. Her grandmother's house looked like a natural disaster had swept through the place, emptying its contents onto the floor.

"It's like someone shook a snow globe," Tosh said. "Is anything missing?"

"I have no idea," Lacy said. Among her grandmother's possessions, she was clueless. She only had a vague idea of what belonged where. "I'll check my room."

"I'll go with you," Tosh volunteered.

Lacy had thought the living room was bad, but then she reached her bedroom. It was unrecognizable. The mattress had been flipped, the drawers dumped onto the floor, and all her clothes thrown from the closet.

"Is anything missing in here?" Tosh asked.

"I don't think so," she drawled, taking a cursory glance at the mad jumble. The only two items of value she owned--her laptop and

127

her phone--were safely inside the bag on her shoulder. To be sure, she slipped it off and looked inside. And then she froze.

"I think I know what they were looking for," she said.

"What?"

"These." She pulled out Barbara Blake's journals and laid them on her bed.

"Oh, this is bad," Tosh said. "We should call the police and make a report."

"I suppose," Lacy said listlessly.

"You don't want to?" Tosh asked. Absently, he picked up a journal and flipped through it.

"Jason is on duty. I think he's had enough drama from me for one morning."

"Maybe they'll send someone else," Tosh said hopefully.

"There is no one else," she answered. "One patrol officer at a time is on duty, and if they need backup they call the state patrol."

"That's crazy and dangerous," Tosh said. "Even in a town this small bad stuff can happen sometimes."

She shrugged. "Budget crisis. Last year half the force was fired. It's a wonder Jason survived the cut."

"Still, I really think you need to fill out a report," Tosh said.

She nodded. He picked up her phone and dialed. She was glad he was taking care of things. Her mind felt numb with shock. At some point she would need to put the house back together, but not now. Now she sat on her bed staring dazedly at herself in the mirror. Beneath her, the possessions that had been haphazardly torn asunder made for a lumpy seat, but she barely noticed.

Tosh finished the call and sat down beside her, settling his arm comfortingly over her shoulders. They sat together in silence until the front door slammed.

"Lacy?" Jason didn't wait for an answer before bounding down the hallway to find her. He stopped short in the doorway and frowned. "Are you okay?"

"I'm fine," she said.

128

Tosh removed his arm. Jason came forward and sat on Lacy's other side. "What time did you leave this morning?"

"A little before seven," she answered.

"And have you been back here before now?"

She shook her head. "I just got home."

Jason checked his watch and she looked at the clock on her bedside. It was almost one.

"Did they take anything?" he asked.

"No. I think they were looking for these, and I had them with me." She pointed to the journals.

Jason released a sigh of frustration. "Who else knows you have these? Besides him." He glanced sharply at Tosh who frowned in return.

"No one. I haven't told anyone. There's no one else to..." She broke off, staring thoughtfully at the journals. "I was reading them at the coffee shop this morning."

"Who saw you?" Tosh asked the question and Jason shot him a quelling glare.

"Just the regulars and no one under the age of seventy."

"Who specifically?" Jason asked. "Anyone you know?"

"My grandmother's group of friends came to talk to me, and so did Mr. Middleton."

"Please don't tell me you think there's an elderly crime circuit in this town," Tosh said derisively to Jason.

"At this point I think it's better if I don't tell you what I think," Jason said.

"What should I do next?" Lacy interrupted before things could get more tense between the two men.

"First I think you should get rid of those journals," Jason said.

"I can't do that," Lacy said.

"That's pretty much what I thought you would say," Jason said. "At the very least we need to fill out a report." He pulled out a clipboard, form, and pen and began writing, asking her questions and writing down her answers.

"I should make myself useful," Tosh said. He stood and began straightening Lacy's room, shuffling papers and putting drawers back in the dresser. "Um, what should I do with these?" His shocked, amused tone caused Lacy and Jason to look up. A pair of delicate black panties dangled from his fingertip.

"Tosh," Lacy exclaimed.

Tosh gave her a mischievous smile. "I guess I see why your name is Lacy."

"What are you...Put those down. You can't touch her underwear," Jason blustered. "What kind of pastor are you?"

"The male kind," Tosh said. He tossed the underpants on a pile of other clothes. "Maybe I should go tidy up in the living room."

"Who is that guy?" Jason asked when Tosh left the room. "Where did he come from?"

"Chicago," Lacy said.

"No, I mean, don't you find it strange that he shows up here now?"

"Now when the church is in need of a pastor? Yes, the coincidence is chilling."

"That's not what I'm talking about, and you know it. How much do we really know about him? Tell me this: Did you tell him you were going to search the murder house on the night you were attacked?"

"Yes," Lacy said.

Jason's eyebrow rose as if to say "See, I told you."

"Jason, Tosh did not attack me that night, and he didn't ransack my room today."

"How do you know?"

"Because I've been with him all day, and because he could have looked at the journals at any time. All he would have to do is ask and I would give them to him."

130

"Why?" Jason said, growing more agitated by the second. "You met him three days ago, Lacy. Why is he suddenly your new best friend? Why are you so comfortable with him? Why do you trust him so much?"

"I don't know," Lacy said. "I just do."

"That's really annoying," Jason said. He stuffed the report back into his binder and zipped it closed.

"What are you talking about?" she asked.

"I've been busting my hump for the past month just trying to get you to look at me, and you're as closed up as a sick clam. Then this guy waltzes into town and you're suddenly pouring out your life story to his waiting ears. Please tell me why you trust a stranger you met three days ago instead of a guy you've known since you were five."

"I guess because if Tosh and I had grown up together, we probably always would have been friends. He would have been in the band with me." Tosh was cute, but not so much that he was intimidating. He was tall and slightly gawky, like a puppy who hadn't quite grown into his paws yet; certainly he lacked the graceful and powerful build of a natural athlete like Jason.

Jason stared at her unblinking, anger flashing in his eyes. "You're telling me that the reason you and this guy are attached at the hip is because ten years ago you might have been in band together?"

"Well, yes," she said. She folded her hands demurely in her lap.

"That makes no sense to me."

"Of course it doesn't, Jason. You never would have been in the band."

He reached out and pressed his palm to her forehead. "Are you having some sort of delayed shock reaction? Your pupils aren't blown, but I could call a squad if you think you might need one."

Impatiently, she batted his hand away. "You can't understand because you've always been one of the chosen ones."

"Chosen ones? Is he trying to recruit you into a cult? Is that what this is about?"

She put her hands on his shoulders and shook him slightly. "You're not listening to me. You were the king of our school. You had no idea what it was like to hope that you were at least in the middle of the social ladder. There's a certain simpatico among outcasts and geeks."

He mimicked her pose, resting his hands on her shoulders. "Lacy, high school was over a long, long time ago."

"For you, maybe."

"What's that supposed to mean?"

How could she explain to him that there was a part of her that would always feel like the chubby girl with braces and glasses? Though she had eschewed social status in high school, always pretending she couldn't have cared less, she did care. Rejection had not only stung, it had scarred. Always in the back of her mind she found herself categorizing everyone she met into which group they would have fallen into in high school. And if they fell into a category that Lacy didn't like, she kept her distance. Though Jason had never said or done anything cruel to her, some of his friends had. There was still a part of her that believed he was going to wake up and realize he was now friends with the girl who played first clarinet in the marching band.

Some of what she was feeling must have shown on her face because his eyes softened, and so did his hands. They slid closer together on her shoulders and his thumbs began making gentle circles on her collarbone.

"Do you know what I see when I look at you?" he asked.

"No," she whispered, barely daring to breathe.

He smiled. "Maybe I'll tell you sometime." His radio crackled to life, reminding them both he was still on duty. "That's my cue to leave. Are you going to be okay? I can come back later."

"I'll stay as long as she needs me," Tosh said from the doorway. Lacy wondered how long he had been there. Had he heard their discussion about him?

"Pardon me if that doesn't make me feel better," Jason said. To Lacy he added, "Call me if you need anything at all. I can be here in less than five minutes from anywhere in town."

"Thanks, Jason, but I'll be fine."

"She'll be fine," Tosh echoed.

Ignoring him even when he brushed by him in the doorway, Jason left the house without another word.

Chapter 15

Tosh stayed for the rest of the day, helping Lacy put her house back together. When it was finally finished, they had a pizza delivered and sat on the couch, eating together in silence.

"Cleaning is exhausting," Tosh said. "I don't know how maids do it."

Lacy's eyebrow rose. "Don't you know this from cleaning your own place?"

He reached for another piece of pizza, avoiding her eyes. "Now is probably a good time for me to tell you I'm filthy rich. Today marks the first time I've ever cleaned a room in my life. And, before you ask, I have a cleaning service for my house. It's not the same as a live-in maid, but they do a good job."

"You're rich?" she said. "But you're so normal."

"Have the other rich people you've known had horns or telltale facial ticks?"

"I've never known any other rich people besides my ex-fiancé, Robert. And that wasn't even him, just his extended family. I mean, probably in New York I brushed elbows with some wealthy people, but I've rarely ever talked to anyone with money before." She sat back, studying him.

"Stop staring at me," he said. "You're making me feel like a freak. You're not going to treat me differently now, are you?"

"That depends," she said.

"On what?"

"On whether or not you're going to start tying pastel sweaters around your neck and talking about your polo pony like rich people in the movies I've seen."

"If I promise not to turn into a character from a Fitzgerald novel, can we please forget the fact that I have a trust fund?"

"Okay," she agreed. He was so down to earth, she was certain it would be easy to do. But now her earlier conversation with Jason came back to haunt her. How could she say Tosh was more her style when he was incredibly wealthy? "Tosh, were you ever in the band?"

"No. I wanted to play the trumpet, but I had braces that kept cutting my lip whenever I tried."

"Did you play sports?"

"I just told you I wasn't cool enough to be in the band, and you think I was somehow a jock?" he asked. "I played video game sports and tried to pretend that made me an athlete."

"Okay," she said, relaxing once again. Rich or not, Tosh was her kind of people.

"I saw some games when I was cleaning that closet," he pointed behind her. "Do you Scrabble?"

"I do, but I'm a writer. Words are my business. Are you sure you're up for the challenge?"

"Try me," Tosh answered.

The game quickly became cutthroat and lasted a long time. When it was finally finished, Tosh suggested they play Monopoly.

"It's midnight," Lacy pointed out.

"I have a few more good hours left before I get really tired," Tosh said, and then he yawned.

"Tosh, what are you doing?" she asked.

"I don't want to leave you here alone," he said.

"I'll be fine, really. You should go."

He looked uncertainly toward the door. "I could stay and sleep on the couch."

She laughed. "That would certainly go over well for the new pastor. You're very sweet to offer to stay with me, but I'll be fine, really. And I couldn't bear it if you got in trouble because of me. In fact, you should make a lot of noise when you leave so the neighbors will know it. Give yourself an alibi for the inevitable gossip our friendship is going to cause."

"I'm not worried about gossip. I'm worried about you," he said.

"I'll lock the door behind you and go straight to bed," she promised.

He hesitated another minute before finally standing and walking to the door. She followed. They stepped onto the porch and turned to face each other. "Call if you need anything."

"I will," she said.

"I can be here in five minutes."

"I know."

"I really think maybe I should stay," he said.

"Tosh, go." She gave him a light shove toward his car. "Whoever it was didn't find what he was looking for, and I don't think he'll come back. I'll be fine."

After another indecisive look toward his car, followed by a yawn, he finally turned in the direction of the driveway. She waited until he was in his car and then she went inside, taking care to lock the handle as well as the bolt on the door.

Strangely, she didn't feel ill at ease. Maybe because what she told Tosh was true, that she didn't think whoever it was would come back, or maybe because she was simply too exhausted to care. Too many nights of going to bed late and waking up early were having their effect. After making quick work of her nightly routine, she stumbled down the hall, fell into bed, and was instantly asleep.

When she woke, she was disoriented. At first she thought it was morning and her alarm had sounded, and then she realized the room was still dark and she hadn't set her alarm.

Something had woken her, but what?

And then she heard it--the telltale creak of the loose floorboard in the living room. Someone was in the house.

Panic immobilized her, causing her brain to freeze and stop functioning. What should she do? Call the police? Where was her phone? With a sinking feeling she remembered she left it in the living room. The nearest landline was in the kitchen, also down the hall and adjacent to the living room. The nearest exit was also on that end of the house, meaning Lacy was trapped with no form of communication.

She had two choices: she could either remain here as a sitting duck, waiting for whoever was out there to come to her, or she could be proactive and either try to call for help or make her escape.

Rolling out of bed as silently as possible, she groped around for a weapon, found an umbrella, and brandished it over her head. Maybe she wasn't making the smartest move, but taking control felt more comfortable than sitting still and waiting for the unknown. With any luck she would be able to slip by the intruder unnoticed in order to make a break for it.

With that thought in mind, she tiptoed down the hallway, her bare feet barely making a sound on the plush carpet. The house was small. She was so close to the door she could taste freedom. All her focus was on the exit just ten feet away, and that was a big mistake. Instead of pausing at the end of the hallway to sweep the room, she stepped in, leaving herself fully exposed.

A hand grasped the umbrella, using it to pull her fully into the room, and then she was against the wall, her wrists held firmly in a death grip.

"What are you doing? Are you trying to get yourself killed?" Jason hissed. The weight of his body pressing her into the wall kept her toes a few inches off the ground.

Lacy's insides went from stark terror to boiling anger in an instant. "What am *I* doing?" she whispered. "What are *you* doing? Why are you in my house?"

"I just got off work and came to check on you."

"That explains why you're still in your uniform, and not why you broke into my house," she said. She was thankful he was still in his uniform; his bullet-proof vest provided a sturdy barrier between him and her thin cotton nightgown.

"I didn't break in. The door was unlocked. What were you thinking not locking it?"

Strange how instantly and completely her panic returned. "Jason, I did lock it. I checked it a few times just to make sure."

He froze and looked at her, his body tense and alert. Instinctively, they both turned and looked toward the hallway, straining to hear any sound.

"Is there an exit back there?" he whispered.

She shook her head. "No door and the windows are painted shut."

He turned so she was flattened against his back instead of his chest. Then he unsnapped his hip holster and placed his hand on his gun. Edging against the wall, he crept toward the hall. When he reached the hall, he pulled out his gun, put it around the corner ahead of his body, and took a step.

At the same moment, a body exploded from the hallway, propelling itself desperately toward the doorway. He tried to get around Jason. Lacy put her hands over her eyes and peeked through her fingers, thinking she was going to witness a shooting in her house, but Jason body-blocked him, holstered his gun, and used his foot to do a leg sweep, seemingly all in one motion.

Though the intruder was on the floor now, he wasn't done fighting. The next second Jason was on top of him, and they were performing what might have been a wrestling match if they were wearing singlets.

At first Lacy wondered if she should intervene. Should she try to hit the guy over the head with something? But then her anxiety began to ease. He was smaller than Jason and unskilled in a fight. Unless he had a hidden weapon, he was no match for the officer who was now on top of him and cuffing his hands behind his back.

He squealed with pain as Jason wrenched his arm and dug his knee into his kidney.

"Are you going to be good, or do I have to hobble your ankles?" Jason asked.

Lacy had no idea what that meant, but apparently the intruder did. "I'll be good, Jason, Please, just get up. I can't breathe."

Once Jason was satisfied that the handcuffs were secure, he sat back and shifted his vest, trying to get a deep breath. The suspect lay on the floor and from the sniffling sounds he made Lacy wasn't sure if he was hyperventilating or crying. Maybe both.

"What are you doing here, Bryce?" Jason asked after a few seconds of silence.

"I thought this was my grandma's place. I walked in by mistake," the guy said.

"You mean you picked the bolt and the hand lock on accident?" Jason asked. His tone dripped sarcasm.

"You know this man?" Lacy interjected.

"He's not a man. He's a kid, barely out of high school," Jason said. "He's a petty thief."

"Hey," Bryce interjected. "I'm not petty."

"And you're not too bright, either," Jason said. He turned to look up at Lacy. "He's generally a violent person unless he's on something." Turning back to Bryce, he grabbed a large handful of his hair, pulled his head up, and looked at his pupils. "You on something tonight, Bryce?"

"No, I swear," Bryce said.

"Why are you here?" Jason asked.

"It was an accident, just like I told you."

"You know who's in jail tonight?" Jason said. "Big Ed. I arrested him myself a couple of hours ago. Are you two still fighting over that money you owe him? Because I think he needs a roommate. You want to stay with Big Ed?"

"No," Bryce yelled, sounding like he was on the verge of crying again. "Please, Jason, I didn't do nothing wrong. I wouldn't hurt her, you know that."

"Then what are you doing here?" Jason asked. "The truth."

"Someone hired me," Bryce mumbled after a moment of silence.

"Who?"

"I don't know. They found me on this internet site a buddy of mine set up. It's like Craigslist for people who need something illegal done, you know? It's anonymous."

"What did they want you to grab?" Jason asked.

"Some books. I tried to get them earlier, but I told them I couldn't find them. I was real nervous about it because everyone knows she's your girl, but they wanted me to come back tonight. They said she had them with her, and I would need to get them while she was here. I was just going to get in and out with the books, I swear. I didn't even touch her computer."

Lacy's computer was on the floor beside her bed. If he knew about it, then he must have been in her bedroom. She shuddered, and Jason scowled.

"Who hired you?" he asked again.

"I swear I don't know," Bryce said.

"Bryce, you lie when you breathe. How do I know you're telling the truth now?"

"I swear on my mother's grave," Bryce said.

"Your mother's still alive. I arrested her two nights ago for possession," Jason said. "Come on; let's go." He stood and began hauling Bryce to his feet. Bryce started to cry in earnest this time, turning a wet face to Lacy.

She blanched when she saw him. As Jason had said, he was nothing more than a kid. He looked too young and too innocent to be a criminal.

"Please, Lady," he pled. "I didn't do nothing. I wasn't going to hurt you. Please don't press charges."

"Don't talk to her," Jason commanded, dragging Bryce toward the door.

"Jason, maybe I..."

Jason held up a hand to cut her off. "Don't even think about it, Lacy. I'm arresting him, and if you won't press charges, then I will. I'm going to take him to jail, write a report, and then I'll be back." He paused at the door and turned to face her. "Will you be okay?" His tone was softer when he looked at her.

She nodded. "I'll be fine."

He nodded once and walked outside, shutting the door behind him. Lacy waited until he started the car before allowing her knees to give out. She sank into an ungraceful heap on the ground, shaking so hard her teeth chattered.

Twice today someone had been in her home. What was so important in those journals that someone had hired a known criminal to retrieve them? It was time for her to find out.

When she went to her room, the sight of her computer made her feel queasy with fear. How long had Bryce been there? Had he watched her sleep? Had he touched her? She shivered again and set her teeth to stop them from chattering. As quickly as she could, she pried up the loose floorboard in her closet, pulled out the journals, and went back to the living room.

Though it was a warm and muggy night, she was chilled with fright. She wrapped herself up in the afghan and opened the first book.

There were three journals, and they were in date order. The one she had already started reading was the newest. She knew this both by the pristine condition of the book and because the items listed were items that were currently in Barbara Blake's home.

The next book she tried listed items that were popular in the seventies, such as Gloria Vanderbilt denim. If she hadn't been so exhausted and frightened, Lacy might have laughed at the thought of the older woman coveting the latest and greatest designer blue jeans.

After quickly sifting that book, she decided it wasn't relevant because Barbara had lived in New York during all of that time. With a tingle of anticipation, she picked up the last and oldest journal. Its pages were already starting to turn yellow, and many of the items listed Lacy had never even heard of, but they had old-sounding names that made her think they were from the fifties and sixties.

She puzzled over the order of things for a few minutes before realizing the books were in reverse order. The last entry in the book was actually the first item Barbara had apparently received, and it was an easy one to figure out.

"The Flakes- one house."

Lacy paused, wrinkling her nose in disgust. Barbara had inherited her house from her parents, the Blakes. Her code for her parents was unflattering, but simple to break. She wondered if receiving the house was significant in some way. Had Barbara channeled her grief over her parents' deaths into trying to acquire more things? Maybe inheriting the house had been comforting to her during her time of distress and she had learned to associate receiving gifts with feeling good.

With no one around to corroborate Lacy's psychoanalysis, it would remain as theory, but she liked to think she was correct. Even though she had never met Barbara, Lacy preferred to think she had a few redeeming qualities. Surely she couldn't be as bad as everyone said she was. Maybe her seemingly compulsive need to have people give her things had to do with trying to fill an emotional hole rather than because she was a manipulative shrew.

The next entry was more cryptic. "Round Hole- Matherly."

The third entry was stranger, still. "Matherly- Bundle."

Then there was a series of entries grouped together, as if they were a unit: "Prim- watch, spoon, radio, chain. Radish- wooden box, vase, silver fork, picture frame. Strings- crystal bowl, thermometer, pen, camera. President- lamp, linens, paper, rattle."

There was a space and then one more entry: "Baker- Gave Bundle for 10." After that there were several blank pages before the entries started again.

Lacy set the journal aside and sat back on the couch. These entries had occurred while Barbara Blake lived here, she was sure of it. But what did they mean? And what, if anything, did they have to do with her murder? How was she supposed to figure their meaning with nothing else to use as a clue?

142

Her last, desperate hope was her grandmother's group of friends. So far they had been reticent and unhelpful when Lacy requested their help, but maybe if she showed them the journal they might be willing to help her decipher it for old time's sake. Or maybe for vindication. The journals didn't paint Barbara in a good light; they showed her as the calculating user people had accused her of being. Perhaps if Lacy came at if from the angle of exposing Barbara's past, her former friends might be more forthcoming.

She yawned, dozed, and jerked awake with a start. She wanted to wait up for Jason; she wanted to see him, to reassure herself that he was whole and still in one piece after his dogfight on her living room floor. And she wanted to try and think about the mystery of the journals some more.

Reaching for the remote, she turned on the television and sat back to watch an infomercial, mentally pleading with Jason to hurry up and come back.

Almost two hours later, Jason wearily let himself in the front door, rolling his eyes when he realized Lacy had forgotten to lock it after he left. No doubt she had felt safe since he had Bryce in custody, but what if whoever hired Bryce had also hired someone else? And what if he was less scrupled than Bryce? What if the next guy hurt Lacy or, worse, killed her?

Jason wiped a hand over his face, feeling the first signs of telltale stubble. He had been on duty for sixteen hours, and, because of budget cuts, he would only be paid for eight. Right now he wanted nothing more than to assure himself that Lacy was okay and then go to sleep.

As he suspected, she had fallen asleep. He paused and smiled at the sight of her curled up in the fetal position on the couch, an afghan draped over her shoulders. He removed the afghan and placed it more fully over her body, leaning in to kiss her cheek. She stirred, hunching into a tighter ball. He froze until he was sure she was back asleep, then took off his shirt and vest and laid them over

143

the back of the couch. He barely had the energy to turn off the television and crawl into the waiting recliner. Almost as soon as he sat down, he was asleep.

Chapter 16

The next morning, Lacy wanted to cry with frustration when she woke just after the sun came up. Why, after years of loafing during college and on weekends, was she suddenly unable to sleep in?

Her peripheral vision caught sight of someone in the recliner beside her. Either her subconscious already knew Jason was there or she expected him to be because she wasn't surprised by the sight. Intrigued would be a better word.

He looked just as good asleep as he did when he was awake. He still wore his uniform pants, a t-shirt, and his boots. Thick, black stubble lined his cheeks and chin, and his long charcoal lashes fanned his cheek, turning his usually devilish good looks cherubic.

She wondered if she should wake him and send him down the hall to her room so he would be more comfortable, but didn't want to disturb him. She did risk covering him with her afghan and removing his boots, though. How he could sleep in work boots was beyond her; he must have been absolutely exhausted when he finally returned home last night.

As evidence to his exhaustion, he didn't stir when she unlaced his boots and removed them from his feet. Lacy resisted the temptation to linger, watching him a while longer. Instead she went down the hall to the bathroom, took a shower, and put herself back together.

She was pale. She had always been pale, but emotional trauma or exhaustion made her seem paler. Now she looked almost translucent, especially with the dark circles under her eyes that spoke of her lack of sleep. A dusting of powder and a smattering of lip gloss were her daily routine, but today she was going to have to go the whole nine yards with blush and eye shadow. Usually when she spent so much time on her makeup, she also straightened her hair for some special occasion, but not this morning. The weather was humid; if her hair remained straight for five minutes, it would be something for the record books. Instead she scrunched it as it dried, allowing her waves to pull into spirals. It wasn't her favorite look, but at least she was embracing the humidity instead of fighting it.

Jason was still asleep in the living room when Lacy tiptoed to the kitchen. The two rooms adjoined, so she tried to be as quiet as possible as she prepared a pot of coffee. When the coffee was finished, she poured a cup and took it to the living room. Even though Jason was asleep, remaining in the kitchen felt lonely. She resumed her position on the couch and reread the journal while she sipped at the warm brew.

"Do I smell coffee?" Jason asked.

When Lacy looked up, his eyes were still closed, but he was smiling. "How do you take it?" she asked. "I'll pour you a cup."

"Cream and sugar," he replied.

She was surprised, but she didn't say so. Somehow she thought tough-guy cops always took their coffee black. When she returned to the living room after retrieving the coffee, he was sitting on the couch. She sat next to him as he reached for his coffee and inhaled.

"I used to hate coffee before I became a cop," he said. "But then you start working so many crazy hours it becomes a necessity."

"I've always liked coffee," she said. "Neither of my parents drink it. I picked up the habit from my grandparents."

"You're really close to your grandma," he stated.

"I'm probably closer to her than I am to anyone on earth," Lacy said.

"Why? Is something wrong with your parents?"

"No. I love my parents, but I've always had a special relationship with Grandma."

"You have a little sister, too, don't you?"

She wrapped both hands around her mug and stared at the murky contents. "Yes I do."

"Is she as close to your grandmother?"

"No, she's closer to my parents."

146

He read something in her tone, but he didn't press the matter. He just wanted to have a nice, normal morning with her without any arguing or tension.

"Did it ever bother you, being an only child?" she asked.

"I wasn't always an only child," he said, surprising her. "I had a little brother. He died when I was five, the year I started school."

"Jason, I'm sorry. I had no idea. What happened to him?"

He lifted one shoulder in a shrug. "One night he had a sore throat, and the next morning he was gone. It was a freak case of Quincy; his tonsils swelled so much they cut off his airway in the night."

"That's horrible. That must have been devastating."

He shrugged one shoulder again, and she understood the subject was closed.

"So we're both oldest children," she mused into the silence.

"I guess that explains why we butt heads so much," he said.

"I thought it was because you were wrong all the time," she said.

He squeezed her knee and leaned back against the couch, smiling at her. "You look very pretty today."

Lacy wasn't expecting a compliment. She felt her cheeks heat with a blush. "Thank you." She, too, leaned back against the couch. They regarded each other in silence a few minutes. Not for the first time, she was regretting her "no kissing" rule when Jason spoke.

"This is nice," he said. "Just to sit here and talk without any pressure. I'm enjoying this friends thing."

"Yes, it's super," she said, stuffing down her disappointment. Apparently she was the only one thinking about kissing. "Want some breakfast?"

"I'll cook this time."

"You cook?" she asked in surprise.

He gave her a knowing smile. "It kills you that I'm blowing up all the stereotypes you've harbored about me, huh?"

If only that were the case. While he was tied up in the neat little package she had created for him, he was safe. But when he started to challenge the precepts she had constructed, he became dangerous. How was she supposed to deal with a guy who saved her life one night, cooked her breakfast the next morning, and was still obviously grieving the little brother he lost twenty years ago?

He used six eggs to make two omelets that were just right-- light, fluffy, and filled with the perfect amount of cheese.

"Where did you learn to cook?" she asked.

"A guy's gotta eat," he replied.

"Your girlfriends don't feed you?"

"Occasionally." He flipped the omelet in the pan and placed it back on the burner. "But I prefer to be self-sufficient."

Lacy pillowed her head on her arms, resting her arms on the table. He was aggravatingly mysterious, and he wasn't supposed to be. He was supposed to be simple. She had always thought him straightforward--athletic guy who likes action and girls. Now he was morphing into someone else. Finding out he was afraid of commitment hadn't come as a shock; she had always assumed he was afraid to be tied down. Finding out he was afraid of everything else was a huge surprise. Jason liked things simple and predictable, like his job, for instance. He seemed terrified to buck the system and stand on his own, even though Travis had told her he was well-liked and respected, a shoe-in for the next promotion.

She also hadn't expected him to be a loner. In high school, he had always been surrounded by a bevy of adoring fans, both male and female. The girls wanted to date him, and the guys wanted to *be* him. She had assumed that since he continued to live in their hometown his life would still be one non-stop party. But he was straight-laced and serious and very much alone. And not just alone but lonely, she realized with astonishment. He was a loner who didn't like to be alone, as confusing as that thought was.

The insecure part of her thought Jason wanted to be with her for his own amusement. She was new and therefore interesting. But

148

maybe he wanted to be with her because the alternative was to be alone.

"Where are your parents?" she asked. "I haven't heard you mention them."

"They moved away a few years ago," he said.

"Do you ever see them?"

"Occasionally," he said. He plated their omelets and set them on the table.

He was being very cagey about his life. She would have called him on it, but he looked so happy. And that was what had been missing since her return- Jason's happiness. Now that she understood the contrast, she realized he had been subtly sad since her arrival. She continued to study him, owl-like, wide-eyed and unblinking, until he looked up and returned her stare.

"What is it?" he asked, his fork paused in midair. "Is the omelet bad?"

"No, it's great. It's perfect, in fact. I've never made an omelet this good in my life."

"Then dig in, Red. I like to see a girl who enjoys her food."

His command had the opposite effect of causing her to eat. "What did you call me?"

"You heard me."

"I don't think I did because my hair's not red; it's strawberry blond."

He dropped his fork and picked up a lock of her hair, holding it in midair between them. "Red."

"Jason, I know what color my hair is." She jerked her head, removing her hair from his grasp.

"You're in denial. What's so bad about red, anyway?"

"Nothing. I've known a lot of perfectly nice redheads. I'm just not one of them."

"Don't sell yourself short; you're nice enough."

"Maybe you're colorblind," she said. "What color is your hair?"

"Brown," he said.

"See? That proves it. Your hair is black."

He chuckled. "Lacy, you're crazy. My hair is dark brown."

"It is not. It's black." She reached her hand up and sifted her fingers through his hair. "In fact, I think I see some spots that are going gray up here. Brown hair doesn't do that at such a young age."

She expected an argument, but he was strangely silent. She looked at his face, now very close to hers, and froze. She watched while he set his fork on his plate and pushed it out of the way, and then he reached for her. His left hand pushed her hair off her shoulder while his right hand settled on her waist.

"How are you after last night? We never really talked about it," he said. His left hand remained at her shoulder, twining in her hair. She felt a little ridiculous with her hands still stranded in his hair, but for lack of a less-awkward resting place, she left them as they were.

"I was shaken up after you left, but I'm fine now."

"Lacy, you have to admit this has gotten out of hand. I think it's time to get rid of the journals and give up this crazy pursuit."

"Not until my grandma's name is cleared," she said. "Try to understand, Jason."

"I do understand, but I'm worried about you. Try to understand, Lacy." He smiled at her and plunged his left hand into her hair at the hairline, his thumb gently caressing her jaw.

Somehow that small gesture changed the tone of things between them. The tension that had been absent all morning returned full force. Lacy tried to swallow, but her mouth was dry. She thought covetously of the orange juice sitting just a few inches away. Maybe if she had something to drink she wouldn't feel so odd. Maybe she wasn't really attracted to Jason; maybe she simply had low blood sugar.

The phone rang, but she made no move to answer. The machine picked up, and Tosh's voice spoke.

150

"Lacy, it's me. I was thinking maybe you and I should spend the evening together so we don't break our streak. Plus, I'm worried about you. I think I should have stayed last night. Call me back so I know you're still alive. I can't believe I'm talking to an answering machine; I feel like I just went back in time. Later."

Jason slowly sat back, removing his hands from her as she withdrew from him. They finished their eggs in silence and he downed the remainder of his juice before he spoke.

"Let me just say one more time, and for the record, that I don't trust that guy."

"Why not?" Lacy asked.

"There's something not right about him. I'm not buying his whole peasant pastor routine. He's not what he seems."

That much was true; Tosh wasn't a peasant, he was stinking rich. But Lacy didn't feel like she should share Tosh's story with Jason. Not only because it felt like gossip, but also because she sensed that learning Tosh was wealthy would make Jason dislike him more.

"He may be unorthodox, but his heart is sincere," Lacy said.

"How do you know, Lacy?" Jason asked.

"I just do," Lacy answered. For reasons she didn't understand, she was uncomfortable talking about Tosh to Jason or vice versa.

"Fine, I'll let it go. It's your life." He drummed his fingers on the table a few times. "So are you going to go out with him tonight?"

"I don't know. I have a lot to do today."

"Like what?"

"I want to gather my grandma's friends together and ask them to try and help me make sense of Barbara Blake's journal. What are you going to do with your day off?"

"How did you know today is my day off?" he asked.

Because since I arrived home I've been watching you obsessively. "I'm observant, I guess."

"Well, I was going to see if you wanted to spend this evening with me, but it sounds like you have a previous invitation. I suppose I could still ask you out and make you choose."

"Friends don't play head games on each other," she said.

"All right, I won't make you choose." He leaned closer and picked up her hand, gently toying with her fingers. "But if I did, which one would you pick? The stranger you barely know, or the guy you've known since kindergarten?"

"I find it interesting that you think longevity would be the deciding factor," she said.

"If not longevity, then what?" he asked.

In answer, she gave him an enigmatic smile before standing to clear the dishes.

Chapter 17

Two hours later, Lacy found herself sitting on Gladys Smith's sofa, shifting uncomfortably every time the plastic covering stuck to a new area.

The entire group of friends was there: Rose, Gladys, Janice, and Maya. Lacy felt awkward without her grandmother as a buffer. She had never spent much time alone with the other women, instead always seeing them at some church function, usually a funeral. Now they faced her in a semicircle of silence, as if she were the teacher and they were awaiting her lecture.

"Thank you for meeting me today on such short notice," she began. "As you know, Grandma is still in jail. I tried talking to the detective about her alibi, but he wouldn't listen."

"What's her alibi?" Maya asked.

"She baked me a prune cake during the time of the murder."

They nodded together. Only a group of like-minded baking grandmothers would understand how much time and effort went into baking a scratch cake.

"I'm sure things will work out," Janice said weakly.

"Frankly, I'm beginning to have my doubts," Lacy said. "The detective in charge doesn't want to listen to reason. He wants to blame Grandma, and he won't investigate any other possibility."

"That's preposterous," Rose said, dabbing at her lip with her ever-present hankie. "Everyone knows Lucy is the kindest, gentlest soul on the planet. She's never done one regrettable thing in her life."

The three other women shifted nervously in their seats. Lacy thought if they had been close enough, they might have jabbed their friend in the ribs with their elbows. Instead they darted her quelling glares until she relaxed into her chair, subdued and silent.

"I agree with you," Lacy said. "But I also feel like it's up to me to make Grandma's case and prove her innocence. That's why I called you here this morning. I need your help." She pulled the three journals from her bag. Was it her imagination, or did the tension in the room heighten a few notches as the four women leaned forward and focused their gazes on the books.

"I found these in the course of my investigation," Lacy said. When no one commented, she continued. "They seem to be some sort of record of things people gave her, but the names are in code. Here, for instance." She opened the oldest book, flipping to the back, and began reading.

"'The Flakes- house.' Obviously they were her parents because I know they left her the house, but these other entries are a mystery. Do they mean anything to you?" She passed the journal into the group and watched while they huddled together over the book. After a minute of silent perusal, Janice slammed shut the book and handed it back.

"No, not a thing. We have no idea. There's nothing in those books that's familiar to us. I have no idea what any of it means. It's a mystery. There's no telling with Barbara. She was an odd bird. Could be anything. We have no idea. She probably became mixed up in something bad in New York."

Lacy blinked at her. "Okay," she drawled. "It's just that everything started and ended here. I can't help but feel like this town is connected with her death, and I think something in these journals might hold the key."

The four women remained silent, staring frozenly at Lacy as if she were holding a gun on them.

"Maybe if you took another look," she began, but Maya cut her off.

"We don't know anything," she said.

"Do any of the names ring a bell with you? Are there any clues that might help me figure out who these are talking about?"

"She did like to give people nicknames," Rose squeaked.

"Rose!" The other three women hissed her name and turned to look at her.

Lacy's mind was beginning to fill in the missing pieces of the puzzle. "Did she have nicknames for you four?" she asked, focusing all her attention on Rose.

Rose nodded. A tear trickled down one cheek.

Lacy glanced at the book, skipping to the section she knew by heart. "Prim--that's you, isn't it, Rose?" Rose didn't answer, but from her baleful look Lacy knew she had guessed correctly. "President, is that you, Maya?" Her maiden name had been Grant.

Maya nodded, her lips pressed tightly together in mute defiance.

"And Strings, that must be Janice." Janice's maiden name was Harpest. "I guess that means Gladys is Radish. Why, though?"

"She said it rhymed," Gladys snapped, the anger in her tone revealing just how much she had hated the nickname.

"I don't understand. Why did you keep this from me? From what I've been able to learn, lots of people gave her things."

Rose's tears increased, and now the other three women looked in danger of joining her. "We didn't give her those things from our own houses," Rose said. The other women tried to shush her again, but she hurried on as if, now that she started, she had to get it out. "We stole them."

Lacy tried and failed to hide her shock. Besides her grandmother, these four were the most upstanding and law-abiding people she knew. "What happened? Tell me the whole story," she commanded, and for some reason they complied. Piece by piece, person by person, they began to tell their tale.

"We were friends all the way through school, and Barbara was always our leader. None of us really liked her, but we were all too afraid of her to leave the group. For a long time she controlled us through verbal abuse. Anyone who crossed her became such an outcast that school was unbearable. It wasn't until her parents died that she really flew off her rocker.

"It started small--the hints for things she wanted from the store. None of us can figure out exactly why we started giving in to

155

her demands, but eventually we did. And then it became a weird game of one-upmanship. Who could steal the biggest and the best item for her? We were all out of our heads.

"I don't know how it would have ended if Barbara hadn't suddenly packed up and moved away. When she left, it was as if a spell had been broken and we all returned to our senses. You have no idea how ashamed and afraid we were. We knew if anyone found out what we did, our reputations would be ruined forever and we would go to jail. We vowed to keep it a secret and never tell anyone. We promised never to break the law or do anything bad again. We went on with our lives and pretended nothing had ever happened. We all got married and became respectable women again.

"And then Barbara returned," Rose finished bitterly. "She sent us notes saying she had proof that would send us to jail."

If they hadn't been so upset, afraid, and downright pathetic, Lacy would have laughed. "But surely you know the statute of limitations on theft is very low. Even with concrete proof there's no way you could be prosecuted after fifty years. And who do you think people would believe? A notoriously bad woman or four upstanding women of the community who are pillars of their church?"

They looked at her, considering. "I guess we never thought of it that way," Gladys said. "Oh. Oh, dear. We've acted very rashly." She pressed her hand to her mouth and looked away, tears slowly leaking down her cheek.

Lacy wanted to tear her hair out in frustration. "What? What else aren't you telling me?" Surely they weren't about to confess to Barbara's murder, too, were they? Was protecting their reputation so important that they would kill to keep the journals covered up? And then with that question she had her answer. "Oh. You hired Bryce to come to my house and steal the journals."

Rose nodded. She looked miserable; they all did.

"We're sorry, Lacy. We tried to get a criminal we knew wasn't the violent kind. We just wanted the journals. If he had gotten them the first time when he broke into her house, then you wouldn't have ever even known about those blasted things."

A new horror began to dawn on Lacy. "So you mean you didn't just hire him to break into my house, you hired him to break into Barbara's house, too."

Janice nodded. "But only after her death, and we had nothing to do with that."

"No, you don't understand. Bryce and I were in Barbara's house at the same time. He hit me in the head and knocked me out. He could go to jail for assault. I could go to jail for breaking and entering. You could go to jail for hiring him in the first place."

"But we hired him on the internet," Maya said. "He never saw us."

"Those internet sites are easy to trace," Lacy said. Bryce wouldn't confess his part in the first attack, but Jason knew. Once they ran the internet trace, the entire story would be in the open. Detective Brenner would learn her part in breaking into Barbara's house. He would love nothing better than to throw the book at her. Everything was about to hit the fan in a big way.

The four women blanched. Rose moaned and Gladys swayed. "What are we going to do?" Janice asked, sounding small and helpless.

"Stay calm," Lacy said, trying to take her own advice. "Things might still work out." The key to everything was Jason. If she could convince him to drop the charges and let Bryce go, then no one would ever be the wiser about her break-in or the four elderly friends' hiring of him in the first place. "I'll work on a solution. Just stay silent and, for goodness sake, don't do anything else."

"Never again," Rose vowed. "We promise never to break the law again."

The vow lost some meaning when Lacy realized it was probably the second time in her life she had taken it. But, statistically speaking, she only had a few years left. That alone might guarantee that she would actually stick to her promise this time.

There was one final thing she had to know before she left. Taking a deep breath, she forced herself to ask the dreaded question. "Was my grandmother in on it with you?"

The other women looked at each other in surprise. "Why, no, of course not," Gladys said. "She was two years older than us and not in our group until much later. And, knowing Lucy, if she had heard about what we were up to she probably would have had us in church confessing before the entire congregation."

"Could she have found out what was going on?" If her grandmother had gone to Barbara's to try and plead her friends' case that might explain the connection.

"No. None of us would ever have told her; we would have been too ashamed," Rose said.

After reassuring them and swearing them to silence and inactivity a few more times, Lacy left feeling exhausted and dismayed. Was no one trustworthy anymore? No one besides her grandmother, that is. Lacy hated to admit it, but there was a large part of her that felt proud her grandmother hadn't been involved in such licentious activity, even if it had happened some fifty years ago.

Her stomach rumbled, reminding her it was lunchtime. She drove through a fast food restaurant and, on a whim, ordered enough for two. Crossing her fingers that she would find Tosh at his church, she let herself in and knocked on his office door.

"Come in," he called and looked up with a welcoming smile when she opened the door. "Lacy, this is a great surprise. But I thought we were on for tonight."

"I can't make tonight," she said. "I have something else to do." Wearily, she sank into the chair across from him and resisted the urge to put her feet up.

He leaned forward with a concerned frown. "Is everything okay?"

"Can I ask you a pastor question?"

"Yes. Do you want me to put my collar on?" He reached for the drawer beside him, but she stopped him with a laugh.

158

"No, that's okay. I want to talk like friends. I just meant I have an ethical dilemma, and I need your advice."

"Go ahead." He crossed his hands on his desk and prepared to listen intently.

"Do you think it's ever okay to cover up a crime?" she asked.

"Are you talking about your break-in at the Blake house the other night?"

"How did you know?" she asked, astounded by his perception.

He shrugged. "Call it pastor's intuition. If you're asking if it's okay to cover up what you did to avoid getting in trouble, then the answer is no."

"But I thought you agreed it needed to be done," she said indignantly.

"I did, but that doesn't mean you shouldn't be willing to accept the consequences of your behavior. You had a compelling reason to break into that house, but it was still against the law. If you get caught, then you need to be willing to pay for your crime."

She digested that and realized she agreed with him. Covering up her actions didn't feel right. If she was arrested, then so be it. "But what if you're covering a crime to protect someone you love?"

He froze and quirked an eyebrow. "Jason?"

She frowned. "Of course not." With a sigh, she unloaded the entire story she had just learned from her grandmother's four friends. When she was finished, Tosh laughed.

"I know I shouldn't find it funny, but it's not every day a pastor learns that four of the oldest and most conservative members of his congregation are actually criminals."

"Tosh, you can't tell anyone," she said, suddenly afraid she had said too much.

"Of course not," he said. "What happens in this office is confidential." He sat back and laced his hands behind his head. "You've raised a difficult question, Lacy. Is it ever right to commit or cover a crime in order to protect the person you love? My first

159

inclination is to say no, but life is full of gray areas. I honestly don't know."

"I thought pastors were supposed to know all the answers," she said.

He shook his head. "Pastors are supposed to know where to *find* all the answers," he replied. "And I do, but it's going to take some time while I study my bible and pray about it."

Tosh was possibly the only person she knew who could say that in a sentence and have it sound sincere.

"That doesn't help me much; I need answers now."

"Here's my advice to you: you have a good head and heart. Use them."

"I have been accused of possessing a tender conscience," she admitted.

"You call it conscience, I call it God. Whatever the case, listen to that inner voice and you'll know the right thing to do when the time comes." He sat up and leaned forward again. "Are you sure you're busy tonight?"

She nodded.

He sighed. "I guess I'm going to have to go out and actually meet some more people in this town. Do you know any other single women you could set me up with?"

"There's Peggy at the coffee shop. She's never been married, and I'm fairly certain she still has all her own teeth."

"Do I detect a hint of jealousy?" he asked.

"No. Peggy's free to go out with whomever she wants."

He laughed. "And what are you going to be doing this evening while I'm wooing Peggy with prunes and arthritis cream?"

"I'm going to talk to Jason." His smile faltered, and she hurried on. "About the things you and I were just discussing. I'm going to try and convince him to let Bryce go."

"Do you think it will work?" he asked, sounding slightly mollified.

160

"I don't know, but I have to try. I don't think sending four old ladies to jail is the right thing to do."

"There's a chance that might not happen. They could cop pleas and avoid jail time."

"But their reputations would be ruined," she said.

"Maybe they should be," he argued. "You could have died if Bryce had hit you any harder. They had no guarantee that he wouldn't hurt you or kill you. They did something wrong."

"Yes, but they did it to *me*. Doesn't that mean I should be able to forgive them if I want to? And they had no idea what they were getting into. They were naïve enough to feel invisible on the internet. They're way over their heads here."

"So are you, but I think you're very sweet and merciful. It gives me hope that you'll extend the same grace to me someday if I mess up."

"I probably would, but there's one way to know for sure," she said.

"What's that?" He picked up her hand and brought it to his lips, bestowing a kiss on her palm.

"Don't mess up," she said. She gave his hand a squeeze and let herself out of his office.

Chapter 18

Lacy worked hard to make herself look good for her evening with Jason. After her breakup with Robert, she had purged most of the things that reminded her of him, but there was one thing she was unable to get rid of: her little black dress. He had liked the dress and always complimented her profusely when she wore it. That alone would have been reason enough to do away with it except for the fact that she liked it, too.

It was perfect--not too revealing, and not Puritanical. It hung exactly right, highlighting her curves without looking like an invitation to explore them. Somehow it could either be dressy or casual, depending on what she wanted it to be. Tonight she was aiming for casual, and with her ballet flats and low-key jewelry she succeeded in hitting the right note.

After securing her hair in a loose chignon and touching up her makeup, she was ready to go.

Jason lived in a small house on the far side of town, which was another surprising thing about him. They were only twenty five. Lacy couldn't imagine owning a house yet, especially not by herself. When she was financially able, she planned to move to an apartment for a few years until she either got married or decided it was time to buy. Apartment living went with the carefree lifestyle she imagined Jason to have. A house seemed so...stable and traditional--two words she hadn't previously associated with Jason Cantor. But she was learning there was more to him than met the eye, even though what met the eye was so appealing one was tempted to linger there forever.

Lacy knocked on the door and stood waiting nervously for Jason to answer.

"Lacy," he said, blinking at her in surprise as he looked her up and down.

"I decided to take you up on your offer tonight," she said, trying to feign a confidence she was far from feeling.

162

He closed the door, blocking her view into the room. "Oh, I wish I had known. I'm sort of busy." He threw a furtive look over his shoulder.

Lacy wanted to shrivel up and die. Why hadn't she called first? "Oh, that's okay, I was just in the neighborhood, and I…" She trailed off and turned toward her car, hoping a rescue would miraculously appear there.

Jason chuckled. "I'm teasing you." He opened the door wider. "Come in." He didn't move aside. Instead he raised his arm, forcing her to duck under. When she was right beside him, he dropped his arm like a bar, trapping her between him and the door. "I feel a little silly," he said.

"Why?" she asked, trying hard to breathe through her mouth so she wouldn't have to inhale his mind-numbing cologne.

"Because I thought you looked as good as possible in running shorts. I should have withheld judgment until I saw you in a dress."

It was happening again. Lacy felt herself almost swaying toward him, as if she were being drawn in like a fish on a line. She couldn't do this tonight; she needed all her faculties to have a rational conversation with him. But then she looked down and saw his charcoal gray t-shirt conforming to his magnificent chest, and some of her resolve wavered. She also noticed a dish towel slung over his shoulder.

"Did I interrupt you in the middle of something?" she asked, hating how her voice emerged as a faint squeak.

"I was doing the dishes," he explained.

"You do the dishes?"

He smiled. "Did you think I have a maid?"

Was that a casual question or a subtle dig at Tosh who did employ a maid?

"Have you eaten?" he asked. "I was just about to grill something."

"You don't have to cook for me," she protested. "We could go out. My treat."

"I was under the impression your funds were limited right now," he said.

Lacy's pride prickled. "What makes you say that?"

"You live with your grandmother and you don't own a car."

"I love my grandmother, and I enjoy walking," she snapped.

"Okay. You're rolling in cash. My mistake."

She relaxed, realizing how uptight she sounded. "Sorry. Funds are a little tight right now. Money is a sore subject. But I'm going to make it."

"I know you will," he said.

His confident tone caused some of the anxiety constricting her chest to ease a little bit.

"Everyone thought I was crazy to leave my editing job in New York," she confessed. "It paid well."

"Did you like that job?"

"It was good," she said.

"Are you where you want to be and doing what you want to be doing now?" he asked.

She laughed humorlessly. "Are you kidding me? I'm scraping bottom."

"If you liked your job there and don't like it here, then why did you come back?" he asked.

Somehow she had stumbled right into the one topic she wanted to avoid. "Sometimes you just need a change, you know?"

"No," he answered. "I have no plans to ever leave here."

"Why? You could have done anything."

"I'm doing what I've always wanted to do." Now it was his turn to look cagey and uncomfortable. Lacy thought it was a good thing their friendship was temporary and would most likely end when she moved away. It wasn't destined to get off the ground if neither of them was willing to open up to the other.

Jason opened the fridge and pulled out a large steak.

"Can I help?" Lacy asked.

"Sure. I'll take care of the meat. You can do the side dish."

164

"What do you want me to make?" she asked.

"Surprise me."

She couldn't believe he was giving her carte blanche to search his kitchen, but she was soon to be disappointed by what she found. His possessions were Spartan and neatly arranged, offering no surprises.

"You're very clean," she said.

"Thank you," he replied.

"I'm not sure that was a compliment."

"I am," he said. "Tidiness is a virtue."

She paused in her search for a vegetable, turning to him with a smile. "Jason, you're such a boy scout." Her amused tone held a hint of wonder. He wasn't turning out to be anything like what she had thought. Before tonight she would have thought his bachelor pad was a hovel, lined with pizza boxes and empty cans.

"You think so, Lacy?" Jason asked, his tone considerably warmer than hers. "Maybe I'll have to change your mind about that." His glance fell to her lips, and then he picked up the platter of meat and headed outside.

How does he do that? Lacy wondered. She opened the freezer and stuck her overheated face inside. While there, she noticed some steak fries and mixed vegetables so that when Jason reentered the house and asked her what she was doing, she was able to pull out the food and hold it up for his inspection.

When he left again, she arranged the fries on a tray and popped them in the oven, then found a pot for the vegetables. Her grandmother had a secret white sauce recipe she always used for vegetables. Lacy crossed her fingers that Jason would have the proper ingredients, and then felt vaguely disappointed when he did. Why would a bachelor have such a well-stocked pantry if not for some female who did it for him? And since he had said his family lived far away, that must have meant that some girlfriend at one time bought him nutmeg and evaporated milk. It was too easy to imagine some female trying to worm her way into his heart and life by setting up camp in the kitchen.

While she was waiting for the food to cook, she also decided to make a dipping sauce for the fries. Because she tended to be a messy cook, she pushed the mixing bowl and ingredients to the far side away from the counter so as not to splash on herself while she stirred.

"Now what are you doing?" Jason slid open the patio and set the platter of steaming meat on the counter.

"You don't have any aprons," she told him. "And I don't want to spill."

He opened a drawer to his right and took out a large dish towel, flinging it open with a flick of his hand. Lacy froze as he moved close and used both hands to tie it around her waist.

"There," he said, not touching her, but also not moving away. "Is that better?"

"Uh-huh," she answered, though now she was in more danger than ever of dumping everything her quaking fingers touched.

"I'll set the table while you finish up," he said. He reached for the cabinet over her head, drawing his body nearer hers so that he was almost but not quite touching her. She was oh-so-tempted to lean back, to give in to the urge to rest her weight against him with no care for what might happen next.

With the plates in hand, there was no reason for him to linger, but he did. His free hand rested on her hip, and his face pressed against her neck, inhaling. "You smell nice," he said, his breath blowing warm on her neck.

Two things Lacy realized right away: First, she had missed this male/female interplay. She had missed touching, loving, and cuddling with a member of the opposite sex. Second, much as she had missed it, she wasn't ready for any of this. Her nerves felt overstretched and on the verge of snapping. At any moment, she was either going to break down into a fit of hysterics or do something equally mortifying like turn and throw herself at him.

166

Thankfully he let her go and turned toward the table. There was something to be said for being with someone who had a lot of experience. He seemed to possess a sixth sense about when to press and when to let things go, unlike Robert who had steamrolled her into every action or Tosh who seemed afraid to make any move at all.

The food was ready and they sat at his cozy kitchen table to eat. The evening was beginning to take on an intimate undertone, and Lacy was beginning to feel the edges of panic creeping in. Her anxious feeling was made worse when she felt his sock-clad feet slip over her bare ones in a gentle caress.

Lacy couldn't believe that not only was Jason playing footsies with her, but that his light and casual conversation gave no indication of the cozy action going on beneath the table. She was torn between appreciation for his technique and chagrin over how many times he must have practiced it on other women.

Her feet had always been sensitive. Robert hadn't liked feet and had never touched hers, even though she would have been delighted by a massage. And now she was practically on sensory overload, trying to come to terms with the fact that Jason was gently caressing her feet while talking about baseball and eating a steak.

"The steak is delicious," was the only coherent thing she could contribute to the conversation for a while. "Do you grill often?"

"The grill doesn't require a lot of finesse. Basically you turn it on, set the meat down, and, voila! it's done. I like this sauce on the vegetables." His big toe pressed against her instep, causing her to lose the thread of the conversation.

"This steak is delicious," she said, then quickly realized she had already said that. Jason must have realized, too, because he looked down at his plate with a smile.

As she groped for more conversation, she spotted a wall calendar with a picture of puppies and kittens. "Do you have any pets?"

"No. My hours are too odd and I'm gone too often."

"So you're just an animal lover?"

At his confused look, she pointed to the calendar behind him. "Oh," he said uncomfortably. "Someone gave that to me."

A girl, no doubt. How many nights had he repeated this scene, cooking for a girl and rubbing her feet under the table? Unlike Lacy for whom there had only ever been Robert. Renewed thoughts of Robert caused her to feel queasy. She pushed back from the table slightly, ending her meal and the under-table foot show.

"Thank you, Jason. I can't remember the last time someone besides my grandma cooked for me, especially not two meals in a row."

"Your last boyfriend didn't cook for you?" he asked.

"Cooking for someone in New York generally means that you order takeout for them," she said, striving for a casual tone. Thinking of how things had been with Robert wasn't doing much to ease her anxiety. She felt on the brink of a panic attack.

Jason templed his index fingers under his chin, studying her. "Was is serious?"

She nodded.

"I've never been serious with anyone," he volunteered. He stood to clear the table and she joined him. He didn't have a dishwasher, so they did the dishes together in silence. Lacy felt the tension mounting between them, and hoped it was her imagination working overtime. They had agreed to be friends, hadn't they? He knew where she stood on the topic of relationships, didn't he? And he had agreed he didn't want anything either, hadn't he?

She began to have her doubts when, as soon as the dishes were finished, he clasped her hand and led her into the living room. He sat on the couch and pulled her down close beside him, keeping hold of her hand.

"I have to tell you that I'm a little surprised you showed up here tonight," he said. "I thought…well, it doesn't matter what I thought. What matters is that you're ready for the next step."

"The next step," she repeated dumbly.

"The next step," he reiterated. His right arm slid behind her back while his left arm eased over her waist, drawing her close enough that their lips were in easy touching range of each other. Then he just looked at her. She had never had anyone else pause that way before kissing her, as if he were savoring the moment. His eyes closed, his head dipped, and that's when it happened. The full-blown panic attack that Lacy had been skittering toward finally erupted.

She pressed her fingers to his lips and blurted the first thing that came to mind. "I think you should let Bryce out of jail."

Chapter 19

Jason paused and kissed her fingers where they lay gently on his lips. "Hmm?"

Obviously he had been too caught up in the moment to hear what she had said. She removed her fingers and eased away from him slightly. "Jail. Bryce. He should go." Now that the initial adrenaline rush was over, Lacy felt drained and confused. How had she ended up in this mess? What signal had she mistakenly given him?

Jason began to come to his senses, too. He dropped his arms and sat back. "What did you say?"

"I said…"

"I know what you said. But I thought I must have heard you wrong. What are you talking about?"

"I don't want to press charges against Bryce for breaking into my house," she said, hoping that would be enough to convey her point.

"You don't have to press charges. I witnessed the crime. *I'm* pressing charges," he said, still sounding confused.

"You can't," she said.

He held up a hand to stop her from speaking. "Wait a minute here. Let me see if I understand what just happened. You showed up here tonight looking like that," he paused to wave a hand at her, "because you want to talk about my job?"

She nodded.

"And if not for that reason, you would be with that other guy right now," he added.

"You make it sound really bad. It's not like that."

"Then, please, tell me what it's like because, from where I'm sitting, you showed up here tonight because you want something from me, and not because you want to be with me."

She sighed in frustration, pressing her fingers to her temples. "No, you're twisting everything around. Tosh and I didn't have specific plans. I had lunch with him this afternoon."

"I'm so glad you could arrange your schedule to fit us both in today," Jason said. His tone was scathing.

"Jason, please just let me explain. You're getting everything all mixed up. I came here because I wanted to talk to you, but that's not the only reason. I mean, I did want to see you; I do want to see you. I was having a nice time until…"

"Until I tried to kiss you. Geez, aren't I the idiot for trying to break that rule? What was I thinking trying to be friends with a woman? It's impossible." He ran his hands through his hair and stood, pacing back and forth a few feet away.

Lacy wanted nothing more than to flee from the awkwardness, but she didn't want to go until she had made herself understood. "Jason, please, you're taking this all wrong. I didn't have any motivation in coming here tonight other than to talk to you."

He stopped short and glared at her. "Fine. Talk away."

It wasn't easy to talk to him when he was scowling at her, but she did her best. "I think you need to let Bryce go."

"We already had this discussion. I'm charging him, end of story."

"But new information has come to light," she said.

"What is it?"

She bit her lip. "I can't tell you."

"You mean you can't trust me. And that's what this is really all about, isn't it, Lacy? You can't trust me because you think I'm the same wild partier you thought I was in high school."

"No, that's not it. But you're a police officer, and what I found out is something that could get someone I care about in trouble."

"Is it Tosh? He's involved in this murder, isn't he? I knew it." He searched around, looking for his phone. "You'd better believe I'm going to arrest him. I'll call it in right now. I can't believe you would want anything less."

"Jason." She stood and practically shouted his name to get him to stop talking and look at her. "What is wrong with you?" she yelled, frustrated beyond control now. "I'm not talking about Tosh, and you are proving to me why I can't tell you what I know. You're so convinced that the law is the law and everything is black and white that you're not willing to look between the cracks at the gray areas to see the people you might be hurting."

"The law protects people, Lacy. The law makes sense of the senseless and order of the chaos. It's the only barrier between some people and total destruction."

She wanted to argue with him some more, but intuition told her he wasn't speaking generally. Her head tipped to the side, studying him. "What happened to you?" she asked softly.

"This isn't about me," he said gruffly. "This is about truth and fact, both of which are on my side."

"And it's also about grace and mercy, both of which are on my side."

They squared off, each one waiting and hoping that the other would relent.

"I'm not going to let Bryce go," he said. "I can't. He broke the law."

With a defeated sigh, she gathered her purse and walked over to where he stood. "Then think about this: When the full truth of what Bryce has done comes to light, Detective Brenner is going to know I broke into Barbara Blake's house. And he's going to make you be the one to arrest me. Are you ready for that?"

He didn't reply; he simply remained silent and stoic, staring at her through narrowed eyes.

She took another step toward him until there were only a few inches between them. "Here's something else for you to ponder: When I eventually am arrested for my role in that night, I won't ever tell that you're the one who found me and that you turned a blind eye

172

to my crime. I would never give you up, no matter what. And I'll be able to sleep just fine tonight. Will you?"

She had to pivot around the coffee table to squeeze by him. Their bodies brushed, and Lacy felt the sizzle on her arm from the contact.

By the time she reached her car, regret was setting in. Regret that she had handled things so badly, regret that she had gone there in the first place, and regret that Robert had left her so broken and bruised that she was no longer whole.

Home was exactly as she had left it, and she was thankful there was no drama waiting for her when she arrived. She simply wanted to get this murder solved so she could get on with her life and get out of this town. And the best way to do that was waiting for her in her room.

After changing into her nightgown and scrubbing her face, she settled into her bed with Barbara Blake's journals. She skimmed all three of them, but kept coming back to her belief that the first one held the key. There was something niggling in her mind just out of reach about the first page, but she couldn't put her finger on what it was, and that frustrated her.

It was a long time before she finally fell asleep. This time she remembered to put her phone right next to her bed in case there was an emergency, but she regretted that action when it rang bright and early the next morning.

For the first time in a while she had been set to sleep in, and then the shrill buzz of her phone woke her from a dead sleep. She fumbled for it, thinking it was an alarm, and not until she heard a man's voice did she realize it was her phone.

"Ms. Steele."

By now she was well acquainted with Ed McNeil's voice. Guessing correctly that she was just about to end the call, he hastened to continue.

"Please don't hang up; this isn't about your grandmother, it's about you," he said.

Lacy's throat constricted with fear. Had Bryce told someone that she was in Barbara Blake's house that night? Was there already a warrant for her arrest?

"What is it?" she asked, her voice shaky.

"I'm handling Barbara Blake's estate," he said.

Uh-oh. If he was the executor, did that give him the power to have her arrested for trespassing? Was that why he was calling, to rub her nose in his newfound power? "Okay," she drawled. Squeezing her eyes shut, she waited for the inevitable axe to drop.

"You're going to need to come in here and sign the papers."

Bile rose in the back of her throat and she swallowed it down. Apparently he was going to swear out a warrant for her arrest. "Couldn't I just meet you at the jail and save time?"

"Uh, okay, if you prefer. I usually handle wills in my office, but whatever."

Her eyes snapped open. "What?"

"The will. You need to sign the will."

"What?" she repeated dumbly. "What are you talking about?"

There was a long pause before he spoke again. "Didn't you know you're her beneficiary?"

"Who?"

"Barbara Blake, the deceased."

"What are you talking about?" she repeated. "That's not possible; I never met the woman."

"Nonetheless, she bequeathed all her worldly possessions to you; the house, her clothing and jewelry, and a bank account totaling a million dollars."

Lacy choked and dropped the phone. She fumbled for it with shaking fingers, dropping it twice more before bringing it to her ear again. "Sorry," she said. "Mr. McNeil, is this a joke?"

"I never joke about money," he said.

And somehow she believed him. Numb with shock, she was just about to hang up when a new thought occurred to her. "If I hired you to represent my grandmother, how soon could you get her out of jail?"

"By noon today," he said.

"Then do it," she said. "I have some questions that need answered as soon as possible." Questions like why a dead woman Lacy had never met left her all of her worldly possessions.

After hanging up with the lawyer, Lacy looked once more at the journal beside her bed. The answer was in the first few entries-- she was sure of it. But what was it?

"Matherly- Bundle," she read out loud. Then a few lines later "bundle" was mentioned again. "Baker- Gave Bundle for 10."

And then something her brain had been trying to tell her finally became apparent. Nowhere in any of the other journals had Barbara given anything away. That meant that this entry was significant, possibly more significant than anything else.

A theory began to come together in Lacy's mind, but she needed confirmation. She picked up the phone and called Rose, not caring that it was still very early.

"Rose, it's Lacy. I was wondering if Barbara had a nickname for Mr. Middleton."

Rose laughed. "We all had nicknames for Tom Middleton. He was only four years older than us, and our math teacher our senior year of high school."

Lacy gripped the phone tighter. "Math teacher?" she squeaked.

"Yes, he was a whiz at math. In fact, that was Rose's nickname for him: Mr. Matherly."

"They dated, didn't they?" Lacy asked.

"No one ever knew for sure, but we all suspected. All the men were crazy about Barbara, Tom especially. There were a lot of rumors about them right before she went away. We all thought that was why she kept to herself so much there at the end."

"Thank you, Rose," Lacy said distractedly. She was almost certain now, but she needed confirmation, and she knew just where to get it. She rolled out of bed, throwing on a pair of yoga pants and a t-shirt before grabbing her purse and heading out the door.

She jogged to the coffee shop and bypassed the usual line of elderly customers. Mr. Middleton sat at his usual seat beside the counter, sipping his coffee, and reading the paper. He looked up when Lacy breathlessly plopped into the seat across from him.

"Hello, Lacy," he said, his eyes narrowed in concern. "Something wrong?"

"You're my grandfather, aren't you?" Lacy exclaimed. The shock of discovery was too new for her to try and be tactful.

He opened his mouth--to deny it?--but then closed it and slumped forward, appearing to age ten years in those few seconds. "So now you know," he said.

"I know that much, but I want to know everything. Will you tell me? Please," she added when he looked uncertain.

"I told you before that Barbara and I were kids together. She was always beautiful and brilliant, like an exotic butterfly. She had red hair and green eyes, much like someone else I know, although it looks like she colored it blond later in life." He paused to smile at her. "I fancied myself in love with her and, as she grew older, she turned her attention to me, too. The day after she graduated high school, she told me she was expecting. Like the poor dumb fool I was, I thought all my dreams had come true. I bought a ring and asked her to marry me. But butterflies don't change their colors. She said no. She wanted bigger and better; she wanted to go to New York."

He paused again and swirled his coffee. "She said she was going to get rid of the baby. I begged with her, pleaded really, not to do that. I told her the least she could do was carry it through to completion and give it to someone who would love it. For a few days, she kept me on the line, and then, to my astonishment, she agreed.

"Your grandpa and I worked summers together painting houses. I knew he was sterile from a childhood case of measles, and I

176

knew he and his wife were nice people who desperately wanted children. Barbara was good at concealing her pregnancy. She stayed home a lot, which was hard on her, and I stayed with her, which was hard on me."

He paused to give Lacy a wry smile again before continuing.

"People didn't talk about such things back then. They didn't announce babies to the world until after they were born. Your grandma, pardon my saying so, has always been a bit on the plump side, and I imagine that when the baby arrived people simply thought she had hidden it the whole time, as was the custom back then.

"When the time came, the four of us went together to the next county for the delivery. Barbara didn't even glance at her baby, your mother. As soon as she was able, she packed up and moved to New York. Giving Fran up for adoption was the one good thing, the one selfless thing she ever did."

Lacy bit her lip. If the journal was correct, she hadn't done it for free. Lacy was pretty certain that "Baker" referred to her grandmother, and it said she gave ten for the bundle. When Lacy had snooped through her grandmother's things, she had noted an old cashier's check for ten thousand dollars. The check stood out both because it had been saved and because it was a whole lot of money for back then. Still, she had no desire to disillusion Mr. Middleton any further.

"But your grandmother, well, I'll never forget the look on her face when the nurse handed her your mother. Over the years, she's never failed to send me a picture of your mom and you girls. And, in a way, I was able to stay involved in your lives. First as your mom's principal, and then as yours. I think they were afraid I was going to eventually keel over in my office, but I wanted to stay until you and Riley were safely out of school. It was my way of protecting you, I guess."

He took another sip of his coffee, and Lacy swiped at a stray tear.

"Why did Barbara leave me her house?" Lacy asked.

His lips pressed into a tight line.

"Apparently I wasn't the only one keeping tabs on you. I think Barbara had written the family off. And then you moved to New York, and she thought you were the one who was like her. Then she saw you and realized how much you look like her. Maybe she had grown sentimental in her old age, I don't know. All I know is that when you moved back here, she panicked. She didn't want you to be stuck here forever. She hatched a plan to come back here and tell you everything. She was going to ask you to go back to New York with her; she wanted to take you under her wing and teach you everything she knew." He finished with a sneer.

"So Grandma did have motive," Lacy said absently. She hated knowing how panicked her grandmother must have been at the thought of Barbara revealing a secret she had kept from her family for fifty years.

"Your grandmother did not kill Barbara," Mr. Middleton said angrily. "Lucy is a saint. She's the kindest, sweetest, most innocent, loving, and upstanding woman I know. I couldn't have picked a better mother for my child unless I had married her myself."

Lacy blinked at him in surprise. "You're in love with Grandma," she said, dumbfounded.

Mr. Middleton stared into his coffee cup, looking supremely uncomfortable. "Stuff and nonsense," he said. "I'm too old for such things."

"You're never too old for love," Lacy said.

He looked up at her with such desperate hope in his eyes she wanted to cry all over again. "Do you think an old codger like me would still have a chance with her?"

Lacy smiled and covered his hand with hers. "You never know until you try."

"And that would be okay with you?" he asked.

"Who better for my grandma than my grandpa?" she asked with a smile.

Mr. Middleton leaned in and spoke in a conspiratorial whisper. "You always were my favorite."

Lacy laughed, feeling lighter and happier than she had in a long time. Peggy happened by their table with a thermos, holding it out for a refill. Lacy watched her pour, and her short-lived happiness was quickly replaced by reality. The DNA on the plates in Barbara's kitchen had belonged to a man. Mr. Middleton had just as much motive for murder as Lacy's grandmother. Had she uncovered a truth that would set her grandmother free, only to incarcerate her newly found grandfather?

For some reason she thought of Jason. What would he do in this situation? No doubt he would arrest Mr. Middleton. Strangely, Lacy found herself agreeing with him for once. Even though she wanted Mr. Middleton to marry her grandmother and live happily ever after, she realized he needed to pay for what he had done. Taking someone's life should never be overlooked or covered up, even if it was done in order to protect someone else.

"Grandma is getting out of jail today," Lacy said. "I think we're all a little overdue for some clearing of the air. But I know Grandma; she won't talk to me about this. Will you go with me and talk to her?"

"Okay," Mr. Middleton said, looking uncomfortable again.

Lacy's phone rang. It was Mr. McNeil telling her that her grandmother was free. She promised to meet him at the jail to sign some paperwork and receive the keys for her new house, and that piece of information gave her an idea.

"I'll drive," Mr. Middleton said.

He stood and ushered Lacy from the coffee shop and to his car. She wanted to talk to him and ask him questions, like why he had never married in all these years, but she kept silent. Her mind was busy replaying last night's scene with Jason and realizing they were both wrong.

It was as wrong to arrest Mr. Middleton for murder with no thought to mercy as it was to grant him total mercy with no punishment. The right thing to do would be to arrest him and grant some leniency for all he had been through. After all, he had unwillingly given up his daughter and stood on the periphery of her life. Then when Barbara came back to town, he had been threatened with a truth he had kept hidden for most of his life. Killing her had been the wrong response, but shouldn't the undue pressure he had been under be taken into account? Maybe temporary insanity would be the best defense.

Stabbing was not generally considered a premeditated murder, but it was certainly gruesome. Lacy's lip curled as she imagined the anger and brute force it must have taken to stab someone to death with a pie knife, and she found herself feeling a little less sympathetic toward her grandfather.

"Here we go," Mr. Middleton said. Lacy looked up just as they arrived at the jail. "Are you ready for this?" he asked, sounding as nervous as she felt.

"As ready as I'll ever be," she said. Then she opened the door and walked to the jail.

Chapter 20

"Tom," Lucinda Craig exclaimed, looking from her granddaughter to Mr. Middleton in astonishment. "What are you doing here?"

"We'll get to that in a minute, Grandma," Lacy said. "First things first." Reaching across her grandmother, she signed the forms that Mr. McNeil held out for her and took the keys from his waiting fingers. "I take it you'll send me a bill," she said dryly.

"Count on it," he said. And even though he had helped her out, the sight of his slimy smile made her feel the need to take a shower.

Lacy and her two elderly companions turned toward the parking lot. She climbed in the back seat while her grandmother and Mr. Middleton climbed in the front. "Are you okay, Lucy?" Mr. Middleton asked when they were safely in his car. "Did they hurt you?"

"I'm fine, Tom," Lucinda said, laying her hand on Mr. Middleton's forearm. "They were very kind, especially a young man named Travis." She looked at Lacy in the rearview mirror, her eyes twinkling. "I think he's sweet on you."

"We're just friends, Grandma," Lacy protested. Riding in the backseat and denying rumors of romance made her feel thirteen all over again. "Can we please stop at the Blake house before we go home?"

Her grandmother and Mr. Middleton turned to look at her. "What for?" her grandmother asked.

"I just need to check on something," Lacy said.

"But the pastor is supposed to meet us at our house," her grandmother said.

"Tosh?" Lacy said.

Lucinda nodded. "He was supposed to visit me today. When I called and told him about my release, he suggested meeting at the house instead. I can't imagine why he's so anxious to see us." The twinkle was back in her eyes.

Ignoring it seemed like the better solution at the moment. "I'll send him a text to let him know we've changed plans." In fact, she would tell him to meet them at the Blake house. The more support she could get for what she was about to do, the better.

"What do you know about this young man?" Mr. Middleton asked.

"He's very nice," Lacy said.

"I don't trust outsiders," he muttered.

She smiled. "You sound like Jason."

"Jason," her grandmother perked up and turned around. "Who's Jason?"

"Jason Cantor," Mr. Middleton volunteered. "He and Lacy have been spending a lot of time together lately."

Lacy wondered how many other people had been watching her without her notice.

Tosh's car was in the driveway when they arrived. "I was already driving when I received your text," he announced. "You caught me a couple of blocks away." He held out his hand to Mr. Middleton and Lacy's grandmother while Lacy made the introductions.

"You okay?" he asked, turning to face Lacy when the introductions were over.

She shrugged. He put his arm around her shoulders and led her to the house, leaving her grandmother and Mr. Middleton to exchange looks behind their backs.

They all trooped into the entryway and stood facing each other, automatically making a circle in the small space.

"What's this about, Lacy?" Mr. Middleton asked. "I can tell you're up to something."

Lacy drew in a deep breath. "I think it's time we all clear the air a little bit." She turned to her grandmother. "Grandma, I know the truth about my mom's adoption."

182

Her grandmother sagged and stumbled, leaning on Mr. Middleton when he offered support.

"I know things were different back then, but adoption isn't a stigma anymore. It's a happy celebration of chosen families. I'll understand if you still don't want to tell Mom, but I'm glad I know. And I love you just the same; nothing could ever change that. You're still my Grandma, and you always will be. And now I have another Grandpa to add, and I think that's pretty great." She had been young when her grandfather died. The prospect of enjoying another was almost too good to be true.

She turned, smiling, to Mr. Middleton. "But on that note, there's something we have to discuss. I want to know what happened that day, the day Barbara was murdered. Grandma, you dropped off the pie and left. That's true, right?"

"That's the honest truth, Lacy," she said shakily. "I tried to convince Barbara not to go public with the adoption, but she wouldn't be dissuaded. I left here very upset and decided that if our worlds were going to be torn apart, then we were in need of some prune cake." She swiped at her eyes. Mr. Middleton moved closer and put his arm around her shoulders, giving them a squeeze.

"She sent you a note, too, didn't she?" Lacy asked Mr. Middleton.

He nodded curtly. "She did, the darn fool woman. She was always trying to stir up trouble when she was young and apparently some people just never learn."

"Did you come here that night?"

Mr. Middleton looked taken aback. "No. I learned my lesson with Barbara fifty years ago. The less contact with her, the better. No good ever comes of getting caught up in her schemes. When she left here all those years ago, I wrote her off, vowing never to have anything to do with her again."

Lacy could tell he meant it. Mr. Middleton was one of those straight-laced protective people who might be compelled to murder in a fit of passion, but he would never lie to cover it up, and especially not to his own granddaughter.

"Then who ate the pie?" Lacy mused.

Tosh cleared his throat. "Um, that would have been me."

Lacy whirled to look at him, her mouth agape. "What?"

His look and tone were apologetic. "She called and told me she was a member of my congregation and invited me over. She gave me pie, and I left."

"You met her? You were here? Why didn't you tell me?" Lacy asked.

"Because when I was here, she made a pass at me. I ran out like Joseph with Potipher's wife. I was embarrassed, and then when I learned about her reputation I was afraid no one would believe that I had left."

"Tosh," Lacy said, the hurt evident in her voice. "You were here after my grandma. You ate the pie she brought. You could have been her alibi; you could have cleared her."

Now it was his turn to look shocked. "Lacy, I didn't think…I promise you that never occurred to me, or I would have come forward. I'm so sorry." He looked over her head toward her grandmother. "Mrs. Craig, I'm so sorry. Please forgive me."

Lucinda waved her hand. "Don't think a thing of it, Pastor Underwood."

Lacy turned away from him, too overwhelmed to deal with the implications of what she had learned from him. She blew out a frustrated breath and pushed her hair away from her face. "If it wasn't any of you who killed her, then who was it?" she asked.

"It was me."

Everyone turned to look at the newcomer, gasping when they saw her gun.

"Peggy," Mr. Middleton said. "What are you talking about?"

Peggy looked at him and shook her head. "You still don't know, Tom. You never did. You never understood."

But Lacy understood. Suddenly the first entry in the journal made sense. "You're Round Hole," she said.

Peggy's brow lowered and her head snapped toward Lacy. "How did you know about that?"

"I saw it in her journal. 'Round Hole- Matherly,'" Lacy quoted. The tiny entry she had pondered for so many days now finally made sense. Peggy was in love with Mr. Middleton, and Barbara had taken him away.

"She was horrible," Peggy said. "You know why she called me Round Hole? Because she said I was like a square peg in a round hole--I didn't belong. And she made sure of it. She ridiculed what I wore, how I did my hair, and the way I talked. None of the other kids would have anything to do with me, or the teachers, either. Except you, Tom. You've always been nice to me."

"But why did you kill her after all this time?" Lacy asked.

"Because she came back," Peggy said plaintively. "I thought she was out of our lives forever, and then she came back. And where Barbara went, destruction followed. I knew she would try to contact Tom again, and I was afraid he would fall in love with her all over again."

"That wouldn't have happened, Peg," Mr. Middleton said kindly.

"Of course not," Peggy said, beginning to cry now. "Because you're in love with *her*." She pointed the gun toward Lacy's grandmother. "I heard you talking all about it in the coffee shop this morning, and I can't take it anymore, Tom. I can't take watching you eat your heart out over someone who's not me." She swiped at her eyes and leveled the gun on Lucinda, but Mr. Middleton stepped between the two women.

"Peggy, you've always been my best friend. Why do you think I spend every morning in the coffee shop except to see you? You've been the biggest part of my life all these years, and the one constant I could count on. We've spent all our holidays and birthdays together."

"Then why didn't you ever fall in love with me?" she sobbed.

185

"I tried to," he said. "I wanted to. But the heart wants what it wants. I couldn't make myself feel something it couldn't, but I do love you. You know that. Don't do this." He stepped forward again and put his arms around her, securing the gun and taking it out of her grasp. She collapsed on his chest and gave great heaving sobs.

A few minutes later, Jason was there. He walked into the house, gun drawn, and then paused in the doorway, a look of confusion on his face.

"One of the neighbors called me and said she saw some people break in here," he said. His gaze leveled on Lacy and narrowed.

Before Lacy could defend herself, Detective Brenner came puffing up the steps behind him, knocking Jason out of the way. "I knew it. I knew we would find you people here. You're under arrest, all of you."

"Oh be quiet, George, before you bust an artery," Mr. Middleton said. He handed Peggy's gun to Jason, keeping his arm around her and leading her forward. "Peggy has some statements to make in regards to Barbara Blake's murder, Jason."

Detective Brenner stared at the gun in shock while Jason took out a clear evidence bag and slipped the gun inside. The detective's mouth worked up and down like a fish out of water before he turned his beady eyes on Lacy with a gleam of triumph.

"You, Miss Steele, are under arrest for trespassing. Your friend, Bryce, has been singing like a bird. Apparently now isn't the first time you've broken into this house, and you'd better believe I'm going to make the charges stick, no matter what Ed McNeil might have to say about it." He turned to Jason. "Cantor, secure that prisoner and then come back to get this one."

There was a part of Lacy that wanted to hear what Jason had to say. Would he refuse? But on the off chance that he wouldn't, she decided to jump in and save him from saying anything at all.

"You can't arrest a person for entering her own house."

The detective did look in danger of apoplexy when she explained that she owned the Blake house and all its contents.

"As a matter of fact, Detective, you are the one who is now trespassing in my house. I would appreciate it if you would leave. Now," she finished, then crossed her arms as she waited for him to walk away.

He looked mutinous, but he somehow restrained himself from saying another word. Instead, he pivoted on his heel, walked to his car, and squealed his tires as he drove away.

She and Jason looked at each other, locking eyes over Peggy's bent, weeping head. So quick she wasn't sure she hadn't imagined it, he winked at her, and then he led Peggy out with his arm around her shaking shoulders for support.

Lacy sagged against the counter, suddenly drained of all energy. Tosh moved closer, resting his hand on her shoulder, and she tensed.

"Lacy, please," he started, but she cut him off.

"Not now. Just not now. I need some time."

"All right," he said softly. With a final goodbye to her grandmother and Mr. Middleton, he let himself out.

"Lacy, are you going to tell Frannie?" Lucinda asked.

"No, Grandma, I think that needs to be your call," Lacy said. "But I do think she deserves the right to get to know her father, and him her."

Lucinda and Mr. Middleton looked at each other, considering. "I can't imagine what it would do to her to learn the truth after so many years," Mr. Middleton said. "I don't want to hurt her or turn her world upside down."

"What if she gets to know him in a different capacity? As my, er, gentleman friend?" her grandmother said, blushing faintly.

Lacy blinked at the older couple in surprise. "I think that would be just great," she said. But when the initial shock wore off, she felt elated over the prospect, and soon she was hugging both her grandma and Mr. Middleton.

Somehow it was appropriate that in addition to her grandmother's happy ending being released from jail, she should also find her very own Prince Charming. *Now if only I could find mine,* Lacy thought.

Outside in the driveway a car started, and Lacy didn't know if it was Tosh or Jason.

Epilogue

"Are you sure you forgive me?"

"Tosh, I'm sure. Please stop asking me that," Lacy replied as they walked up the sidewalk to Barbara Blake's house. She wondered how long it would take until she stopped thinking of it that way and started thinking of it as her house.

"But I messed up, Lacy. I'm embarrassed by my weakness, and mortified that you had to be the one to see it. I panicked by not telling you everything, and you were so brave and composed throughout the whole ordeal."

She knew these words almost by heart because he had said them to her--repeatedly--and written them on the note he sent with a dozen roses. Twice. They reached the house and she turned to face him. "Tosh, please stop apologizing. It's all over and done. I probably would have forgiven you sooner if I hadn't been dealing with so much at the time. You neglected to tell me you had pie, you didn't burn down an orphanage. It's fine; we're fine."

He took her hand and looked at it, playing with her fingers while he spoke. "You know what the hardest part of being a pastor is?"

She shook her head.

"It's trying to figure out how to be a man, too. People are watching me, waiting to learn by my example. I have to be extra careful not to make the wrong move, to go slowly, to keep appearances as well as actions on the up and up."

"I know, Tosh," she said. "And I appreciate that about you."

"Yes, but how much do you appreciate it?" he asked. "In the kind of way that you tolerate it because we're friends, or in the kind of way that you're willing to be patient with me and wait for things to progress beyond our friendship?"

"I..." The question caught her totally off guard, rendering her speechless.

Tosh pressed his index finger lightly to her lips. "Don't answer that tonight. Think about it." He removed his finger, leaned down, and pressed a light kiss to her lips. "Are you sure you don't want me to stay?" he asked, resting his forehead on hers.

She shook her head and opened her eyes. "No. Thank you, but I really just want to be alone to sort through her things and try to figure out what to do next."

"All right. Call if you change your mind." He grasped her chin with his thumb and forefinger, casting a longing look at her lips, and then he left.

Lacy let herself in her house and made her way to the master bedroom. Pulling out all the shoes from the closet, she looked at the size on the bottom. Apparently she and her grandmother had more in common than their hair and eye color; they had the same size feet. But to Lacy, this wasn't good news. If the shoes had been the wrong size, she could easily have given them away.

But now before her sat thousands of dollars worth of designer shoes that looked brand new. And they were her size. Keeping them felt wrong, but so did giving them away. These items were the only tangible reminder of her biological grandmother. Should that mean anything?

Her phone rang and she picked it up, not paying attention to the caller ID. "Lacy, it's me."

Lacy's heart felt like it stopped beating. "Riley," she choked.

"I have some news, and I wanted you to hear it from me first. Robert and I are getting married."

Lacy tried to swallow and couldn't. "Congratulations," she choked, and then she hung up. Her lips were numb, and the room swam. She lay down, put her feet in the air, and some of the sensation began to return to her extremities.

The doorbell rang and she stumbled down the hall, throwing open the door without looking to see who it was.

"Lacy, are you okay?" Jason asked. She hadn't seen him since the day he arrested Peggy, two weeks ago. She had wanted to call, but

190

she didn't know what to say, and she was afraid of the possible rejection.

She nodded. "Why do you ask?"

"Because you're crying," he said. Taking a step closer, he swiped his fingers on her cheek and held them up so she could see the moisture.

"Oh," she said. She sniffled, and it was as if a dam burst. She put her hands over her face and sobbed. Jason herded her into the house and closed the door behind them.

"What's wrong?"

His gentle, tender tone made everything worse. She cried until she hyperventilated. He searched the kitchen, returning with a paper bag for her to breathe into, and then he led her to the couch, sat, and put his arms around her.

She leaned against his chest, thinking how good it felt to be held.

"Is this about your grandma?" he asked.

She removed the paper bag and laughed bitterly. "It should be," she said thickly. "You would think that after learning my grandma isn't my grandma and that my actual grandmother is dead would have some effect on me, but it hasn't. I'm happy Grandma is home, and I'm happy she's dating Mr. Middleton now."

"Then what is it?" he asked. His fingers trailed softly up and down her arm.

"My sister is getting married," she choked.

"Oh," he said, still clearly confused.

"This is so humiliating," she said. She hunched forward and put her head in her hands again.

He rested his palm on her back. "Lacy, lots of little sisters get married first. You're only twenty-five. There's nothing embarrassing about that."

"You don't understand," she said.

"Then explain it to me."

She looked up at him, trying to think of a way to explain without feeling like a fool and a failure when their eyes caught and held. The atmosphere crackled with electricity. Lacy sat on her knees, scooting closer. Jason froze and watched her as she cupped his face between her palms and drew him closer.

"You said no kissing," he reminded her.

"I said a lot of stuff," she whispered. "It's time to stop listening and start doing."

"Done and done," he said, and then he kissed her.